# THE ARCHER'S SON

# M. E. HUBBS

Illustrated by Tracy S. Lyndon

Cover Designed by Ian LaSpina

Castle Photo credit: Andrei Belaichuk

Maps Created by David Walker

Published by:
Bluewater Publications
1812 CR 111
Killen, Alabama 35645
www.BluewaterPublications.com

# Acknowledgments

I owe a great deal of gratitude to many people who were kind enough to read early manuscripts of *The Archer's Son*. The comments they provided enabled me to hone and craft the story into what it is now. These folks are too numerous to name, and for fear of forgetting someone, I'll trust that they know who they are and that they are deeply appreciated.

I would like to call out two groups of people who contributed greatly to the development of this story, but in very different ways.

The ladies of my local Society of Children's Book Writers and Illustrators (SCBWI) critique group have been essential in keeping me motivated. They provided the nuts and bolts detail for improving parts of this book and other projects.

The ladies and men of the "Days of Knights" living history project contributed more than they can ever know with the knowledge they provided concerning the material culture of the medieval period. To make a historical novel believable, an accurate depiction of the life-ways, clothing and equipment is essential to transport the reader to that time and place. These dedicated men and women are some of the best in the United States at recreating the various personas of medieval Europe. They eagerly and freely shared their expertise, and for that I am truly grateful.

My thanks also goes to artist Tracy Lyndon for the amazing art work that he produced for this book and my previous one. He also introduced me to Angela Broyles, the owner of Bluewater Publications. Without the confidence and hard work of these two individuals, my work could not have made it to print.

I reserve my most fervent appreciation for the most important person in my life. My wife Phyllis is my best friend and fellow traveler, and my most honest critic. She has been my sounding board for story ideas and scene development and has endured reading drafts in bits and pieces for over two years. Our shared love for British history has made this project special for both of us. I owe all of my success to her support, love and patience.

**To Sarah, Kathryn, Lily, Alex and Arianna**

*May good books always be your joy*

## PART ONE
### Rumors of War

*What of the men?*
*The men were bred in England*
*The bowman - the yeoman -*
*The lads of dale and fell.*
*Here's to you - and to you!*
*To the hearts that are true*
*And the land where the true hearts dwell.*

Sir Arthur Conan Doyle
*The White Company*

# CHAPTER ONE

**On the lane to Treween**
**Altarnon Parish, Cornwall**
**7 May 1415**

Hedyn crept toward the dead house that stood crumbling at the edge of the wood. Its pole and thatch roof had long rotted away, and a young oak tree grew triumphantly where a once thriving hearth had been. Some of the stones had been carried away to build other cottages, but it took a brave man to steal from a dead house. The boy caught his breath. Through the gaping door and sagging windows, just for an instant, he saw a face contorted in agony. He shuddered.

Spirits lingered here, spirits of seven long-dead children. The Great Mortality ravaged the village when his grandfather was just a boy. It took these children and many others. Their tiny bones lay beneath a line of seven little piles of stones behind the cottage. If the wind blew just so, a mournful wail would whistle through the crumbling walls that had once been their home. Hedyn, like all the village boys, usually made a wide detour around this or any other dead house he had to pass on his way to the fields. Now he tiptoed to this one, fearful of disturbing "The Seven." He struggled to overcome his fear, for he knew what he must do. He hesitated and went inside.

Several dead houses remained standing in this manor and every other manor in Cornwall and England. Half of all the serfs, freemen, and nobles perished during the Great Mortality. After sixty years the population had yet to recover. Many small dwellings, where whole families had died in agony, stood abandoned. Some remained deserted because of superstition and fear of the dead. Most remained vacant simply because there were too few people to fill them.

Hedyn shouldn't be here. April brought the barley planting, and now that the ground had warmed, his father would have him working in the fields every day. It had been a long winter, which only grudgingly yielded to spring. The sky had remained rainy, the color of lead. He waited impatiently all through the early months of the year 1415 for a beautiful day such as this. He wanted just one day for himself before his father set him to work in the fields. As soon as the dawn revealed a clear sky, he slipped away from his family's cottage with his bow and one arrow.  He only needed a single arrow.  He expected his father to give him a good thrashing for running away from his work, but he didn't care.

*Besides*, he thought, *if I bring home that big hare, all will be forgiven.*

Hedyn stalked the largest hare he had ever seen.  He had spied it the day before as it bounded across the trail far in front of him.  He could do nothing then, as the hare disappeared into the briars near the tumble-down house.  He had no bow with him then, and besides, tenants from the Master's lands accompanied him as they trudged up the muddy path to the fields.  Although many manor folk stole game from Lord Trelawny's lands, Hedyn knew that any one of them might seek favor with Sir John by reporting a poacher.  Young Hedyn had no rights under the law.  He was the son of a villein, a bondsman, a serf.

Hedyn's heart raced as he stepped through the cottage door, certain that bony hands of The Seven would reach for him.  No hands came.  Another step and something tugged at the hem of his tunic.  He gasped, but before terror overcame him, he looked down and discovered that no devilish hands ensnared him; only a thistle entangled the coarse wool of his tunic.

He blew out his cheeks and sighed in relief as he strung his bow.  With one end of the bow's stave on the ground and braced against his left leg, he gripped the top end and pulled down hard.  He strained to loop the end of the cord over the groove on the end of the bow staff.  Hunting hares required no chase, but it required much patience and stealth.  Hedyn would wait for the hare to show himself, and the dead house provided perfect concealment to ambush prey.  He knew that he must use the ruins to get his hare.  A large rift in the ruined walls allowed the boy to see behind the cottage, beyond the graves of The Seven.  He imagined himself sighting through an arrow slit in some distant castle, waiting for his French enemies to appear.

More than anything else, even hunting hares, Hedyn longed for the day when he could leave the manor and see some of the world outside of Altarnon.  Going to war often played into those fantasies.

Hedyn's bow was but a toy compared to his father's.  It was much shorter, and drawing the cord was a trifle compared to a man's bow.  Despite the small size of both the boy and the bow, they made a deadly pair. Like all boys of low birth, Hedyn received his first bow before he was old enough to work the fields or tend the sheep. Archery was more than a sport or means to hunt; the law required it. Males of common families were required to learn the craft, practice it, and be ready to use it against England's enemies. Indeed, archers had become the backbone of English armies, and the longbow struck fear and dread into the hearts of French men-at-arms. The French never came to understand that the longbow was only a tool. Its devastating power came from a lifetime of practice. English archers began training to kill at seven years old.

A flock of rooks cawed loudly and settled into a broad oak nearby. Their noisy squawking drew the boy's attention away from the patch of clover for a moment. When his eyes returned, large ears above the tall grass betrayed the hare munching lazily about thirty yards away. Pulling the cord to full draw on Hedyn's small bow equaled lifting a fifty-pound stone. Yet he hardly felt the strain as he pulled the hemp cord all the way back to his right ear. A novice shooter may have sighted along the arrow's shaft, but Hedyn knew his bow as well as his own arm. He had only to see his target, and, as if by some magic, arrows would follow his will. He loosed, and the arrow flew true.

Hedyn squeezed through the broken wall and tiptoed respectfully through the seven piles of stone. He nervously looked back over his shoulder at the house and the graves but knew that he would never fear them again. This hunt was a victory over his superstitions as much as his quarry.

The hare lay on its side in the grass. Its open eyes were like black glass beads, but they did not see. The arrow was tipped with a blunt wooden knob, so there was no blood. It did its deadly work instantly, and then skipped off into the underbrush. The boy smiled as he pushed the hare into his cloth sack. He retrieved his arrow, its goose-feather fletching marking its resting place in the bracken.

Hedyn, pleased with himself, crossed a narrow hay field and stepped off onto the sunken lane. The trail led south from the village of Treween to his cottage in Penpont. He heard voices coming from up the hill on the winding trail. They were French-speaking voices, in an excited conversation, which he could not comprehend. He stopped and hurriedly flung the game sack far off the trail into the high grass. He dare not try to hide where there were too few trees and bushes to conceal

4

"He loosed, and the arrow flew true"

him. The boy decided he would have to stand his ground, come what may.

Hedyn did not speak French. His English was passable, but he was most comfortable in his native Cornish. Although he could not understand the words, he knew that one voice belonged to Sir John Trelawny. Sir John and his family were the only folk in Altarnon Parish who spoke French. Norman French was the language of the king's court, the nobility, and the landed gentry. Common folk clung to English. The stalwarts in Cornwall, like Hedyn, still spoke the ancient Cornish tongue. It had remained so since the Norman invaders brought the French language with them over three hundred years before.

Sir John held title to almost all of the lands of Altarnon Parish, from Treween to Trewint. These villages housed the freemen tenants who worked the fields. In the middle of them all was Penpont. This collection of dwellings supported the parish church, the Holy Well of Saint Nonna, the corn mill, smithy forge and the archery butts where all the parish men practiced their shooting. Hedyn's family lived in Penpont. They were the last villein family left in the parish. The world was changing. Few serfs remained in bondage on the land.

The clip-clop of hooves came from around the bend. He quickly unstrung his bow and waited by the side of the trail. The boy lowered his eyes respectfully as the horses stopped beside him.

"What have we here?" Sir John said in English. "Are you not Hedyn, my villein's son?"

Eight horse legs confirmed that Sir John had a companion, but Hedyn could not see who sat on the smaller horse on his master's opposite side.

Hedyn bowed slightly. "Aye, Sir John, Jago is my tas... I mean, my father."

"And why are you not working in my fields with Jago?" asked Sir John, his tone matching the sunny weather. The question was one of true curiosity instead of accusation.

"I was practicing with my bow at the archery butts. I am on my way to the field this minute."

Hedyn kept his head bowed as he spoke, hoping his lie would go undetected. He struggled not to look at the game sack. He knew he would be in trouble if his master found it. His eyes remained on the elaborate brocade on the tails of his master's silken doublet. Sir John leaned his head back and roared with good-natured laughter.

"Well, boy, I wager there is not a better thing that you could be doing on this forenoon, not even plowing!"

Sir John's good humor confused the boy, and he stole a glance at his master's face. Sir John smiled at him.

"Hurry to your father, boy. Tell him to come to Saint Nonna's when the sun is highest on the morrow. I've sent word to all of the men of my villages to gather there." Sir John gave heels to his courser and the sturdy horse moved on, leaving his companion in front of the boy. Hedyn looked directly into the eyes of young John, Sir John's son. He grinned at the sight of his old playmate.

"You were no more at the butts than was I, villein's son."

Hedyn's smile faded. Sir John sent young John away four years earlier to serve as a page to the Earl of Devon. Now he had returned home; but this was not the good-natured boy that he remembered playing with on Saint Nonna's green. John glanced up to ensure that his father had ridden out of earshot.

"I brought my father good news today. His happiness has blinded him. No one goes to the butts with a single arrow for practice, and a blunt-tipped hunting arrow at that. You have been hunting my father's hares, villein's son." Young John emphasized "villein." The word left his lips as though it were a curse.

Hedyn opened his mouth to speak but then lowered his eyes. He did not know how to respond. At thirteen, John was only a year older than Hedyn, but the contrast between the two made the difference in age seem immense. John sat high on his young courser. The morning sun reflected on the silver studs that decorated his wide leather belt. He wore a cotehardie of fine embroidered linen. An array of gilt buttons decorated his chest and wrists. Broadcloth hosen and red leather shoes kept the spring chill from his legs.

Hedyn wore a simple, oversized woolen tunic that made him appear smaller than he really was. He looked down at his mud-splashed

7

bare legs. He suddenly felt aware and ashamed of their contrast. He quickly straightened the linen coif over his dark Celtic hair and tied it under his chin. Hedyn found his voice. "I, I am going to my father as Sir John has commanded, Master John."

"Squire John. You will address my person as Squire John. I have completed my training with the Earl of Devon, and I am now a squire until I am knighted myself someday. Your poaching will not be revealed to my father...for now. But as a serf on the manor I will inherit, I will expect loyalty and obedience from you. I will not hesitate to have you flogged if you disappoint. Do you understand?"

The change in young John both startled and frightened Hedyn. He decided a question might mask his fear.

"Yes, Squire John. Squire, what good news do you bring to Sir John?"

John leaned down from his horse and said in a delighted whisper, "News that King Henry is going to war. Sir John will command a company of men from Altarnon."

Hedyn tightened the grip on his bow. His eyes shone with excitement.

"And, villein's son, you and I will be going to war with them!"

Squire John kicked his courser and rode on, leaving Hedyn standing by the lane. He fetched his game sack and retraced his steps toward home. This time he hardly noticed the dead house as he passed it. The Seven no longer haunted him.

# CHAPTER TWO

**Village of Penpont**
**Altarnon Parish, Cornwall**
**8 May 1415**

Hedyn winced and leaned to one side to keep a tender cheek off the rough oak bench.

"Hedyn has a sore arse from his whipping!" Tressa said in English with a giggle.

"*Taw taves hwoer*!" Hedyn replied in Cornish. Tressa was only ten, but her tongue was as sharp as that of the miller's wife. She knew just how to annoy her brother.

"Hedyn, you will not tell your sister to shut up." Hedyn's mother ladled a thick soup of chopped cabbage and barleycorn into the wooden trencher that he shared with Tressa. Hedyn moved his hand to the clay pot of ale they also shared. She snatched it first and took a long draught, cutting her eyes toward him in a silent taunt.

Hedyn glanced longingly at the hare hanging by its feet in a smoke-blackened corner of the crowded cottage. It had been weeks since he had last eaten meat. He frowned at the bland soup in his trencher.

Jago caught his son's eyes. "Eat your pottage, boy. I'll skin the hare after the sun goes down. Your mamm will stew it with some turnips on the morrow. The salt I got from the miller will make it even tastier."

Hedyn could tell that Jago was pleased with the hare and his use of the bow, but did not expect him to say so. Despite the hare, he was punished for running away and neglecting his work in the fields. But Jago showed some mercy. Hedyn was only whipped with rope on the rear end instead of being beaten on the back.

Hedyn looked around the ancient cottage—the same tiny cottage in which Jago was born. As villeins, he and his family were part of the land, just as their ancestors before them. No one could guess how long Jago's family had served the lords of Altarnon. Each time the land changed hands, the serfs who lived and worked there were sold with it.

They were part of the property, just as the fences, the cottages, the trees, and the very soil itself.

"Guen, come and sit so we can say our graces," Jago said to his wife.

Guenbrith took the iron pot off the fire and sat it on the dirt floor. A thin coil of smoke wafted up to curl around the thatched ceiling then escaped lazily through a hole in the roof. She took her seat next to Jago at the little table where she shared a trencher with him. The family bowed their heads.

"Our merciful and compassionate God has given food to them that fear Him. Bless this food, Oh Lord, and receive our thanks. Amen."

They crossed themselves and said little as they finished their meal.

Hedyn scraped the dregs of his meager meal into the pig's slop bucket and asked, "Tas, who do you think Sir John will make commander of his archers?"

Sadness came over Jago's face as he glanced at his son. Jago was not a tall man, but his shoulders were very broad and his arms thick. A lifetime of shooting stout war bows had developed his upper body in such a way that his appearance alone announced that he was an archer. Although he was a villein, he was the most skilled bowman in Altarnon. Indeed, he had proven this by winning the parish archery tournament on three occasions. But for all his strength and all his skill, Jago's arrows would never again taste French blood. His left leg was crooked and stiff. A maddened ox, an overturned plow, and a tangle of leather harness had conspired to break his leg three years before. "I know not who the master will make his ventenar. Denzel Crocker, mayhap. But I would wager on Thomas Kelnystok. He is a fair man and a skilled archer. He would make a good choice."

Hedyn wanted to kick himself for asking. He knew his father was longing to be ventenar, but there was little chance he would be considered. A lame man could not keep up with an army on the move. Hedyn could not bring himself to tell his father that he was to go to France.

Voices passed the cottage. Men were starting to assemble at Saint Nonna's.

10

"Gather our bows and a bundle of arrows. I wager we will spend time in the target butts after Sir John speaks to us this day."

*  *  *

Hedyn was amazed at how many men had gathered near the ancient stone church. He followed Jago's halting steps across the packhorse bridge that spanned Penpont Water. The church was nine hundred years old, one of the oldest in Cornwall. It was established by Saint-Nonna herself, and her stone altar was there yet. Indeed the whole Parish took its name from this holy altar and church.

Many men had brought their families. Children were playing and chasing among the clusters of folk who stood talking on the green. Someone had tied a popinjay high in a tree, and a group of men and boys took turns shooting arrows at the feathered target as it twisted and swayed lazily in the breeze.

The countryside was buzzing with rumors of war. Archers were England's greatest export, and French ransoms and treasure were its top import. Men were willing to risk their lives for well-paid work and a chance to bring home French gold.

The men who hoped to serve as archers leaned on tall bow staves and carried linen arrow bags on their backs. A few men of higher standing carried long swords. They wore an assortment of armor and chain mail, according to their wealth and means. Squire William Laneer owned a tiny manor near Altarnon. Laneer was of a good family with noble heritage, but his small landholding was not prosperous. His tarnished and battered armor had been handed down from his grandfather who fought the Scots many years before. The armor of Jan Tregeagle was new and shiny but very cheap and plain. He was a prosperous tenant on Sir John's lands.

"Does Jan Tregeagle still draw the bow?" Hedyn asked his father.

"No. Tregeagle fancies himself a future squire. He's bought himself armor and a cheap sword. He no longer associates with us lowly bowmen."

Hedyn caught sight of his best friend, Roger Kelnystok, weaving through the crowd to him. Roger had sandy hair and fair skin, with a sprinkle of freckles across his pug nose. He treated Hedyn as any other

11

boy in the parish and never mentioned his tie to the land or questioned why he had no last name. Hedyn could almost forget that he was a villein when he spent time with Roger.

"Hedyn, have you heard? My tas is to be ventenar!"

A bit of light left Jago's eyes and he turned his attention away.

"So, it will be your tas and not Denzel. My tas guessed it, for 'Thomas Kelnystok is a fair man and a skilled archer,' said he."

Roger beamed. "Aye, Sir John told him this forenoon, and I am also to go on campaign!"

Hedyn smiled wide at the thought of him and Roger going to France together, but he said nothing. He wanted his father to hear the news of his going from Sir John himself. Jago's feelings were battered enough without his son rubbing salt into the wounds of his disappointment.

A cheer went up, and Hedyn knew that someone's arrow had pierced the popinjay.

"Look at Tregeagle yonder in his new armor. He fancies himself far above his station now that he has acquired a bit of wealth." Thomas's voice surprised Hedyn. Jago turned and found his friends Thomas Kelnystok and Denzel Crocker standing behind him. Thomas nodded his head toward Jan Tregeagle, who stood with his wife near the edge of the crowd. His sword point was on the ground and his hands rested on the pommel of its brass grip.

"Aye," Jago responded. "I saw him practicing near his cottage with his sword a few days hence. He flailed the air as though the sword were a barley scythe. I feared that he would hurt himself with it."

All three men chuckled. "If he hopes to capture a French noble and gain a great ransom as he boasts, he should choose to fight one that is old and blind. That is the only way he will survive that battle!" Denzel said with a laugh. Denzel's Celtic ancestry showed in his dark hair and dark eyes. He wore a long beard that tumbled untamed down his chest.

Heads began to turn up the hill on the road to Treween to watch the approach of a stranger. The crowd murmured, for few newcomers moved between the manors. A fresh face always interested folk, causing endless gossip and speculation.

"Do you know him?" Denzel asked as he stroked his beard. He had the habit of running his fingers through the course whiskers when he spoke.

"No, but he is an archer for certain," Thomas replied.

The stranger stood tall with broad shoulders. He may have been reckoned handsome by the village women, save for his nose. Some long ago break had left it leaning to one side. Dressed for war, he carried his bow stave in a horsehide case on his back and his arrows in a waxed linen bag on his shoulder. A chain mail hood covered his head and shoulders, and he held a bascinet helmet under his arm. The helmet was smooth-sided with a pointed peak that swept gracefully to the back of the head. Although scoured clean, the steel was battered from long use in combat. His belt supported a short sword and dagger.

"What brings him here do you reckon?"

"To join Sir John's company, of course. If he is chosen, then an Altarnon man will be left behind. Sir John will supply the king with only twenty archers," said Thomas.

"Twenty archers you say, Tom?" asked Jago.

"Aye, Sir John has signed an indenture with King Henry for twenty archers and five men-at-arms."

"Only twenty archers in his company! Not like the day when we marched from Altarnon with five and thirty men to fight for the old King Henry."

"Aye, but all five and thirty did not return from Shrewsbury. We left many good friends buried on that field. Did we not, Jago?"

The stranger stopped to ask a question and an old man pointed to Thomas. The stranger looked up and walked directly to the new ventenar. He had a dour but determined look on his face.

13

"You are ventenar?" he asked as though he had trouble believing that Thomas truly had been given command of the archers.

Thomas was puzzled by the man's contempt. "Yes, I am Thomas Kelnystok and I'm to be ventenar."

The stranger's eyes swept from Thomas's head to his feet as though he was surveying his worthiness.

"Christ's bones, I am too late. Sir John has already made his choice." The stranger shook his head and started to turn away.

"Wait, Stranger. Who might you be?" Thomas placed his fingers on the man's sleeve as he spoke.

The stranger looked down at Thomas's hand on his arm but did not turn back to face him. He hesitated as though he was deciding if he should answer. "William Whitwell of Devon," he said before he walked away and stood apart from the Altarnon men.

Hedyn and Roger looked at their fathers for some explanation.

"That is a hard man. He covets your job, Tom."

"Aye. I hope he shoots as poorly as he makes friends, and then he will not be chosen to go!"

Sir John Trelawny, Squire John, old Father Leofric and Father Stephen emerged from the wide church door. The crowd hushed and gathered close about them. The old priest offered a long, sleepy prayer in Latin that only he, Father Stephen, and God could comprehend. After what seemed like ages to Hedyn, the monotony of the prayer was interrupted by giggles and laughter that moved like a wave through the gathering. A little dog chasing a rat emerged from the forest of legs and disappeared around the church. Hedyn and Roger's laughter lingered a bit too long, and both received playful cuffs on the back of their heads from their fathers.

Father Leofric stopped abruptly and scowled through his gray beard at the interruption. He switched to English. "May

14

Saint Nonna, mother of Saint David, bless and protect us all." He crossed himself and stepped back to stand near Father Stephen.

Sir John Trelawny was known for his skills in battle, not for making speeches. "You know why I have gathered you here. Our sovereign, King Henry, intends to have his lawful inheritance of the throne of France. If that frog-eater King Charles does not yield, then Henry shall lead a great host to Normandy to seize his throne

Hedyn tried to catch Squire John's eye, but his old friend would not look his way. He stood in his new armor with his fancy helmet under his arm, trying hard to look older and more important that he really was.

Jago leaned near Thomas and whispered, "I hear that Henry has no real claim to the French throne."

"Aye." Thomas whispered back. "But he believes he does, and he can afford an army. That is all that matters."

Father Stephen stepped forward. He was a new priest at Saint Nonna's, an Englishman, but respected by his Cornish parishioners. He read portions of the king's indenture, translating from French.

"This indenture, made between the king our Sovereign Lord of one part, and John Trelawny, Knight of Altarnon, of the other part; Witnesseth that the said John is bound to our said Lord the king, to serve him, if it pleaseth God, in his kingdom of France.

And that the said John, shall have with him a retinue of five men-at-arms, himself counted, and twenty horse archers; the said John taking wages for himself two shillings a day. He shall take for wages of the said esquires and men-at-arms twelve pence, and for each archer six pence a day." Murmurs of approval rose from the men in the gathering. Sir John smiled. Father Stephen hesitated to allow the comments to ebb.

"And the said John shall be bound to be ready at the sea, with said people, well mounted, armed and equipped, and that said John shall make muster before such persons as it may please our Lord the king."

Sir John stepped forward. "So there you have it. There will be twenty archers. Pay will be six pence per day, or four pence if I provide your horse. I will take Father Stephen as chaplain, two women to cook, and two boys to follow this company in France. The boys will be Roger Kelnystok and Hedyn, son of Jago."

Jago looked down at Hedyn with astonished eyes. "So, you are to go, and I am to stay."

Sir John continued. "I will choose the men-at-arms, and I shall have two ventenars." There were questioning looks among the men. No one had ever heard of a company with two ventenars. "Thomas Kelnystok shall be my battle ventenar when we go to France. But, until this company departs, Jago, my villein, will be ventenar. He will direct all training and equipping of the archers for the weeks until we march. No man may challenge his decisions save myself. He will also choose nineteen archers from among you this day. Choose well, Jago."

Denzel slapped Jago on the back. "Well, my ventenar, it appears you have work to do!"

Hedyn turned to his father and grinned. Jago straightened and lifted his chin. He smiled and announced with new confidence, "All men who wish to shoot for a place in Sir John's company, follow me to the archery butts!"

Of all the folk assembled at Saint Nonna's that day, only William Whitwell of Devon wore no smile.

# CHAPTER THREE

**Village of Penpont**
**Altarnon Parish, Cornwall**
**6 June 1415**

"This bodkin will punch through a knight's armor as if it were cobweb." The smithy held the smoking arrowhead up with heavy iron tongs for the boys to see. He slid it back into the coals. The smithy's wife pulled the handle of the great bellows and sent a blast of yellow flames and sparks through the forge. Her charcoal-blackened face seemed even blacker when her smile revealed a few scattered white teeth.

The blacksmith pulled another red-hot bodkin from the fire and thrust it into a wooden bucket of cow urine. Hedyn and Roger wrinkled their noses and coughed when the acrid steam burned their eyes.

When the arrowhead had stopped sizzling, the smithy tossed it from his tongs to Roger, who juggled it from hand to hand. He passed it quickly to Hedyn. The smithy's wife handed her husband a jug. He took a long draught of ale, and then he wiped his mouth with the back of his hand.

"See how I've hammered the steel out to a long four-sided point? After I forge it, I file it to make it nice and sharp with clean edges. Then I reheat it to red-hot and quench it in the cow piss to harden the steel. The hard tip will hole even the best armor out to a hundred paces."

"How many must you forge?" asked Roger.

"Enough for each of the twenty archers to have one sheaf of arrows. Each sheaf holds four and twenty. The king will provide more arrows after Sir John musters with the army."

The boys were in awe of the smithy, as much from his appearance as his skill with the hammer and anvil. His bare arms glistened and bits of ash and dirt stuck to the sweat. At first glance one would have thought his back was twisted from some ancient injury. A closer look revealed that his right shoulder and arm were half again as large as his left, over developed from a lifetime of swinging heavy hammers. Both arms were covered with scars from countless red-hot mishaps, and a large patch was missing from his beard.

"*Clang, clang, clang*, the smithy began to hammer another hot piece of iron into a tapered shape."

18

Hedyn handed him the finished bodkin and he tossed it with a clink into a sack of completed points. He drew another arrowhead from a different sack and held it up for the boys to see.

"A broad head for shooting men and horses," said Hedyn. The swept barbs of the broad heads had always reminded Hedyn of a falcon's wings when it dove down upon its prey.

"Aye, and much more trouble to make than a bodkin. But a good broad head will make a wound that will let out the blood and shred a man's innards. The trick is making them light enough so they fly far, but strong enough so they will not fold when they strike flesh."

*Clang, clang, clang*, the smithy began to hammer another hot piece of iron into a tapered shape. The sound of shouting came from behind the forge, shrill enough to be heard over the pounding of the hammer.

Hedyn and Roger looked at each other and both said "*muskogyon!*" The smithy's wife laughed through a toothless grin as she continued to pump the bellows.

"Aye, another crazy person being taken to Saint Nonna's Well by pilgrims," said the smithy. But Roger and Hedyn did not hear him. They had already turned and run from the forge. The smithy shook his head and laughed.

Saint Nonna's was not a rich church. It had no sacred relics. No piece of the true cross or bones of a saint graced its altar. Pilgrims were few, and it was pilgrims who brought money. But the church did have Saint Nonna's Well, where the blessed saint herself struck the ground to make water come forth nine hundred years before. Some in Cornwall believed that this well had healing powers—powers that could heal the mind. Every week or so, some poor mother or father or husband or wife would bring a troubled person to the church. Father Leofric offered prayers, a few coins would change hands, and the blindfolded *muskogyon* would be pushed backward into the small, deep pond where the waters bubbled from the earth.

The afflicted were only allowed to leave the pond after all traces of madness were gone. This was usually when they began to lose strength from treading water. A cure was promised for all manners of infirmities of the mind: idiots, drunkards, and those who heard voices and saw demons. Once, a rich man from Dunheved threw his daughter into the well to cure her of being a Lollard and straying from the doctrine of the Holy Church. But no one knew if she repented and returned to the one true faith.

The boys crouched behind bushes to watch the cure. Father Leofric and Father Stephen dragged a young man by his arms in the direction of the well. He cried and shouted for help in vain. His mother trailed behind, her head bowed in shame. Father Stephen lifted him onto a stone block as he struggled. Father Leofric gave him a shove, but before he fell, the frantic man twisted and fell face first into the pond with a great splash.

"Well, I guess they wasted their pennies," Roger whispered with resignation. "Won't work if you go in face first. Has to be back first."

"Surely Father Leofric will let them try the cure again," answered Hedyn.

"No, it will be another time, and they will pay again."

They watched in silence for a while as the young man's splashing and cursing began to diminish.

"I don't think it works anyway," Hedyn offered. "I've seen Olfric, the idiot of Treween, thrown in three times, and still he grunts like a pig and cock-a-doodle-doos like a rooster."

Father Leofric reached down to pull the young man from the well but was dragged into the cold water. The boys pressed their palms over their mouths to stifle their laughter. Father Stephen dragged both dripping and sputtering men from the healing well. The priests, the *muskogyon,* and the broken-hearted mother started back to the church for more prayer.

"Serves that old thief right for taking that poor woman's money."

The sudden sound of a loud voice behind them made the boys jump with fright. They turned quickly to find William Whitwell of Devon standing over them. They looked up at him in terror.

"I've met few priests who love God more than money. Most are no better than a Calais cutpurse." Whitwell turned and walked away, leaving the boys sprawled in the bracken.

Hedyn turned and looked at Roger with wide eyes and open mouth. "That man frightens me!" he said.

"Aye. I've heard that he is a hired soldier that serves from lord to lord, wherever he can make a few shillings. My sister heard that he comes from the Scottish marches, where he led a company of men who raided across the border for plunder. And the miller's wife told my tas that he comes from the London highway, where he was a robber and murderer!"

Hedyn pondered this information for a moment, and then asked, "Which is it? Which is true?"

"I know not." Roger brushed the leaves from his knees as he stood. "Mayhap all of them."

"Has anyone asked him?" Hedyn asked as he stood and fell in step beside Roger.

"Are you daft? Who would dare ask him?"

"Where is he living? I see him at the butts practicing his shooting almost every day. He speaks to no one."

"That I know for certain," Roger said with confidence. "He has fixed up a dead house near Trewint. He buys food from the local folk and is waiting for Sir John's company to march."

"Aye, my tas was forced to choose him for an archer, for he was the best shot at the butts that day," Hedyn said.

"There is nothing left to see here. Let us sneak behind the mill and see if we can pinch another fairing from the miller's wife," Roger said with a smile.

Hedyn returned a mischievous grin. His family could never afford the sugar and wheat flour to make the sweet ginger biscuits. "A taste of a fairing would be a treat indeed! Someday we shall get caught, you know."

"But not this day!" Roger broke into a run and Hedyn followed laughing.

They barely heard the mournful wail from the troubled young man as they passed the open doors of Saint Nonna's Church.

# CHAPTER FOUR

**Village of Penpont**
**Altarnon Parish, Cornwall**
**16 June 1415**

"But Tas, I must have a new bow! My old bow is too small for me. How can I go to France without a proper bow?"

"You will need no bow for the work you will do, Hedyn. You'll be too busy fetching water and firewood and all manner of things to serve Sir John. Besides, I don't think you are strong enough to pull a bigger bow."

Jago glanced at Guen and winked when Hedyn was not looking his way.

Hedyn sputtered. His frustration with his father showed on his face.

"Jago, you must cease teasing our son!" Guen shook a wooden spoon at her husband for emphasis.

"If Hedyn should get a new bow then I should have linen cloth to make a new kirtle!" Tressa demanded.

Jago looked at Tressa in her undersized, ragged dress and Hedyn who had puffed himself up in indignation. "Yes, yes, Hedyn will get his new bow, and we will find some means to buy linen for Tressa's new kirtle."

Tressa clapped her hands with joy. A relieved grin spread across Hedyn's face.

"Come, boy." Jago led Hedyn outside to the rear of their tiny cottage. He pushed his hands into the thick thatch under the eaves of the roof and pulled out a long, heavy shaft of wood.

"I've been saving this for some time. As soon as I learned that you would go to France with Sir John, I decided it should be yours. It's Spanish yew wood. The best for making a long bow."

Hedyn couldn't resist and reached to run his hand down the raw wood.

"Why not English yew wood?"

"English yew is good, but Spanish and Portagee yew make the best bows. Turn around and stand still."

Hedyn reluctantly released the yew and turned. He wondered why his father had him face away. Jago stood the shaft against Hedyn's back and measured it one hand's breadth above the top of his head. With a small knife that he carried in his belt, Jago scratched a mark into the wood.

"That will be the length of the finished bow. It will draw much heavier than your old bow, almost as heavy as that of a man. Do you think you can draw the arrow all the way to your ear?"

"Of course, Tas! I am no longer a child."

Jago laughed. "We shall see. I'll have it shaped, nocked, and finished in a few days."

A week later Jago handed the new bow to Hedyn. Guenbrith stood by her husband's side and smiled with pride at her two men. She gave Hedyn a waxed linen bag filled with strong hempen bow cords that she had spun and twisted with her own hands.

"It is indeed a thing of beauty!" Hedyn exclaimed. The yew bow was a single solid length of wood, but looked as though it were made from two lengths of wood joined together side by side. The shaft had been cut where the honey-colored sapwood from the outer tree joined the dark brown heartwood from the middle of the tree.

"Look here," Jago pointed. "The white back of the bow pushes against the dark belly. That makes the release stronger and sends the arrows farther. That is why the best bows are made of yew."

The contrast between light and dark was made even more pleasing with a shiny coating of bee's wax and tallow. Hedyn burst with pride and hugged his mother and his father in turn.

"Now boy, you must string it before you can shoot it."

Hedyn took a cord from the bag and hooked the bottom notch, then braced the staff against his leg. He was used to a much smaller bow, and the top notch where he was to hook the hemp cord seemed far above his head. His hand reached for the tip of the bow and he pulled down with all his might to bend the wood so he could slide the loop to the notch. Jago stood with his hands on his hips and smiled.

Hedyn began to grunt as the wood struggled to keep itself straight. His arms began to quiver and he lost control. The bow sprang from his grasp, leaped into the air, and fell at Jago's feet. Hedyn looked at his father, certain that he would be scolded or be the butt of a joke.

"Pick it up and try again. When you get it strung, come find me in the field."

Hedyn stood looking at his father as he walked away. Guen smiled then turned away and went back to her work.

*How can I ever bend this bow? What will Tas and Roger think of me if I cannot string my own bow?* At first he was angry with Jago for leaving, then thankful that he had no audience as he struggled to bend the yew. His frustration turned to determination, and he picked up the length of wood. The bow seemed to have a will of its own. An hour later, Hedyn's arms and shoulders ached as though he had done a whole day's labor, but he wore a broad smile as he ran to the barley field to find his father.

* * *

"You, villein's son, run to the brewster and fetch ale for the men."

"But Squire, I have no money to buy ale," Hedyn answered urgently.

Squire John sheathed his sword then wiped the sweat from his brow with the back of his arm. He frowned, pulled a silver penny from his purse, and threw it toward Hedyn. The boy made a clumsy catch and set off to the village alehouse.

Sir John had business with the Lord Warden at Dunheved Castle, a morning's ride to the east. He instructed his son, Squire John, to gather his company at the archery butts where the men-at-arms were to teach the archers how to use swords and poleaxes.

"Should the archers find themselves in a tight spot in a fight, they need to be able to defend themselves," he had explained to Squire John.

Only the squire and Jan Tregeagle seemed to take the training seriously. The other men-at-arms were bored, and most of the archers felt that the might of their bows would always keep the Frenchmen at bay. The July day had turned very warm. The men-at-arms sweltered inside their armor. The archers wore no armor, but their quilted jacks and gambesons were just as hot. Their dripping sweat and parched throats made the men even less attentive.

The brewster draped a sack of several clay jugs over Hedyn's shoulder. "Mind those jugs! Don't break them, and be sure to return each one. I have counted them!" Martin Brewster shouted after him as he left the alehouse.

He walked awkwardly with the heavy bucket suspended in front of him, trying to prevent the ale from sloshing out. The rope handle cut into his palms as he carried it with both hands. He was relieved, and a bit proud of himself for not spilling a drop as he arrived at the butts.

"How much of my ale did you spill, serf?" Squire John asked.

He turned his attention away before the boy could answer. Hedyn stood to the side and was ignored by the squire and the rest of the men. He searched his memory to find what he had done to receive such scorn from Squire John. He longed for the days when there was seldom a cross word between them. John only spoke to Hedyn now if there was some task to be given or some insult to deliver.

The squire did not offer him a single drop of the ale. The men dipped the jugs into the bucket and shared them around. Hedyn watched anxiously, hoping for a few swallows. Soon the ale was gone. The men grumbled as they buckled on swords and slid steel helmets back onto sweaty heads.

William Whitwell looked up at Hedyn. The boy shuddered and looked away. He wondered what the big archer wanted of him.

"You did not have a share of the ale, boy?"

Hedyn looked up. "No, I did not."

"Here then, finish this." Whitwell put a jug of ale into Hedyn's hands before he turned and rejoined his mates.

The boy stood silently with the jug for a moment, watching Whitwell as he donned his helmet. Had this frightening man just shown

25

him a kindness?  He had expected a rebuff of some kind, but instead there was thoughtfulness.  He tilted the clay jug and drained it in two long swallows then wiped his dripping chin with the back of his sleeve.

The men lined up once more, and the men-at-arms instructed each archer on the use of the poleaxe, a long wooden shaft with a steel head that included three weapons in one.  A large ax head was opposite a lead-filled mallet.  The ax could chop flesh and the mallet could stun a man through the toughest helmet.  Protruding upward between the head and mallet was a long spike, a half foot long or more.  Hedyn thought that it was the most frightful weapon he had ever seen.  He could imagine the spike piercing armor or jamming through a helmet's eye slits.  After learning basic moves, the men traded their steel for wooden versions of sword and poleaxe before practicing against one another.  Sir John did not want to lose fighting men by accident before they ever faced the French.

William Whitwell stood with a poleaxe.  He held it in the middle of the long shaft and with it positioned across his chest.  He could not conceal the look of boredom on his face.

Jan Tregeagle stood in front of Whitwell, brandishing his wooden sword.  "That's not how you hold it, you big ox!  Blood of Christ, man, did they teach that in Devon?  You know nothing about fighting!  Hold it lower on the shaft so you can get a proper swing."

Whitwell reluctantly moved his hand down the shaft and lifted it high above his head.

"Now come at me with it.  Let us see how you do."  Other men noticed their exchange and stopped to see the lesson.  Tregeagle seemed to enjoy the attention.

"I'd rather not."

Tregeagle beckoned the man with his fingers.  "Come on, bowman.  Frightened of my wooden sword?  I'll try not to hurt you."  Tregeagle lowered the visor on his helmet and stood confident in his cheap armor.  Some of the other men laughed nervously.

"Why do you not attack as I command, you oaf?"  The closed visor muffled his voice.

"The bow is my weapon.  I have no use for the poleaxe."

26

"You wear my patience thin. I shall come at you!" Tregeagle lunged with his sword, and the archer nimbly stepped aside. As the visor-blinded man-at-arms passed, Whitwell twirled his weapon and clouted his opponent on the back of the helmet with the butt end of the shaft. The blow made Tregeagle stumble, but he managed to stay on his feet. A roar of muffled anger spewed from Tregeagle's visor and he turned again to attack. The archer shifted his weapon and rammed it against the charging man's breastplate. Tregeagle came to a sudden stop then started backing up to avoid a series of lighting fast jabs and blows from the wooden poleaxe. Panic was obvious in the man-at-arms' flailing weapon. None of Tregeagle's sword blows made contact with Whitwell, but the crash of the wooden poleaxe on armor came with every retreating step. Whitwell pursued the man until a clump of grass snagged an armored foot. Tregeagle crashed to the ground on his back with a great clatter of metal plates.

In a flash, the archer was upon him with a foot planted on Tregeagle's metal chest. With the end of the poleaxe, Whitwell flipped up the downed man's visor. The panting Tregeagle opened his eyes to see the tip of the weapon an inch from his nose.

"The Devil take you! I...I thought you said you did not know how to use the poleaxe!"

"Nay. I said that I had no use for it. I know very well how to use it."

Whitwell offered his hand to help his opponent rise, but Tregeagle slapped his hand away in disgust. He struggled to his feet with sixty pounds of armor resisting his efforts. There was wide-eyed silence from the other soldiers as Tregeagle glared at Whitwell, and collected his things. His armor clanked as he stalked away. All the men looked at Whitwell, but Hedyn could not tell if their looks were from surprise or from contempt.

Whitwell faced the archers. "This should be a lesson to all. Do not assume any man-at-arms can be beaten thusly. An armored man who is skilled with sword and experienced in his plate will kill you swiftly. But inexperienced men, or men who esteem themselves too greatly," Whitwell nodded his head toward Tregeagle, "are easy marks. Get them to the ground and you can slay them."

He turned his attention to Squire John and his remaining men-at-arms. "Squire, I beg you to never underestimate an unarmored man. He may seem vulnerable because he wears no steel, but he may take your life before you know it."

Squire John blinked and quickly nodded his agreement.

Whitwell noticed the silent stares. "Squire, I think it is best that I take my leave for today." Squire John nodded again and Whitwell walked off to his dead house in Trewint. Denzel Crocker stood by Thomas's side. A low whistle piped through his closed teeth. He put his fingers into his beard and started to say something, but a harsh look from Thomas silenced him.

Hedyn watched Whitwell disappear around a bend in the lane. *There is more to this stranger than we can see,* he thought.

"Thomas Kelnystok, the lessons are ended for this day. Dismiss your archers," said Squire John.

Squire John and his three remaining men-at-arms collected their weapons and departed. Hedyn stood apart and watched as Thomas gathered his men. They talked in low voices. Hedyn could tell they were discussing Whitwell's humiliation of Jan Tregeagle, but he could not tell which way their discussion turned. Soon they dispersed and started for home without a glance at the boy.

Hedyn was left standing by himself. He sighed heavily, gathered the clay jugs, and put them in the empty bucket. As he crossed the packhorse bridge on his way back to the alehouse, he realized that the big archer was the only person who had shown him any kindness that day.

# CHAPTER FIVE

## Saint Nonna's Green
## Altarnon Parish, Cornwall
## 12 July 1415

Half a dozen arrows bristled from the ground around Hedyn's feet. He had often seen his father stick arrows into the ground point first to make them easy to reach for fast shooting. He drew the bowstring back to his chin and then hesitated. He tried to muscle the cord but could pull the stout bow no farther. As he struggled, his arms began to quake. Roger stood behind him coaching.

"Don't stop; draw it all the way to your ear!"

Hedyn loosed the arrow. His trembling arms sent it sailing over the earthen butt and into the woods beyond. He stamped his foot on the ground in frustration.

"It does no good to get cross," Roger said. Hedyn had heard the same from Jago many times before, but from his friend Roger, it irritated him even more.

"Easy for you to say. You don't have a new bow that you cannot draw!" He picked up another arrow, nocked it, and pulled the cord back to his chin. He loosed the arrow before his arms felt the strain. The arrow struggled through the air and struck a fat sack of grass he had set as a target.

"See, you can shoot straight," Roger said without conviction. He knew that the draw was not complete and did not take advantage of the bow's full power.

"When I draw only to my chin, the bow has no more power than my old child's bow," Hedyn said with dissatisfaction. "It could not pierce a woolen shirt, much less armor." The muscles across Hedyn's back and shoulders burned with fatigue.

A clamber of hoof beats, shouts, and whistles rose up from the other side of the little stream called Penpont Water. Hedyn and Roger stood on tiptoes and looked down the road to Dunheve. Soon, a herd of horses streamed across the packhorse bridge. Sir John's new mounts for the march to France had arrived. Hedyn knew that somewhere in the herd there was a horse for his use. Since learning he would have a horse, he had imagined himself astride a large, prancing stallion.

Squire John and Jan Tregeagle rode up to the trees near the archery butts and dismounted. They slapped dust from their clothing and wiped sweat from their faces with dirty cloths. Hedyn's excitement overcame his dread of Squire John. He and Roger approached respectfully and waited until being acknowledged by the squire.

"Squire John, the horses look splendid!" Hedyn said.

"Aye, most are. I have two excellent new coursers that I will be taking. And, I've found just the horse for you."

Hedyn stood straighter and said, "You have, Squire? Thank you!"

"Aye, she is an ancient palfrey with a sway back and a foul disposition. Just right for a villein's son." Tregeagle dutifully laughed at the squire's description of Hedyn's horse.

Tregeagle had become Squire John's shadow. He delivered his messages, ran his errands, and laughed at his attempts at humor. He did anything required to garner favor with the squire or Sir John.

Hedyn's smile faded, but he ignored the insult. "I promise I will take good care of her, Squire John, no matter how foul her disposition."

"There is a palfrey for you as well, Roger Kelnystok."

Roger nodded. "Thank you, Squire."

"Whose bow do you carry?" Tregeagle asked.

"My own. My tas made it for me," Hedyn answered.

"Too big and too fine for the likes of you. Can you draw it?"

"Um, well, mostly." Hedyn looked at his feet.

"As I thought. A waste of fine yew wood. You should give it to a real archer," Tregeagle said with a sneer.

Squire John snorted a laugh, which Tregeagle echoed loyally. They led their horses to the herd grazing on the green. The boys stood silently and watched them move away. Hedyn's disappointment in shooting his new bow was magnified tenfold by the brief encounter with Squire John and Tregeagle.

"Pay no mind to that idiot." William Whitwell looked at the boys as he leaned from behind a tree where he had been sitting. He chewed on the end of a long strand of grass. The boys stared at him in surprise.

"Oh, I have been here for some time enjoying the shade. I felt no need to announce myself to the squire or his lap dog. Come here and let me see your new bow."

The boys hesitated then cautiously approached the big archer. Hedyn handed him his bow. Whitwell ran his hand down the length of the shaft, and then examined the cow horn nocks on either end.

Whitwell looked up at Hedyn. "Spanish yew, I'd wager?"

Hedyn nodded. "Aye, Spanish it is."

"It is an excellent stave of wood, and it has been fashioned into a fine bow. You should be very proud of it. I saw you shoot. You have the makings of a good archer, you know. Do not despair that you cannot yet draw it all the way. It will come with practice."

He handed the bow back to Hedyn. He stood a little straighter and a bit of his confidence returned.

"As I said, pay no mind to that hypocrite Tregeagle. Did you know that he is also the son of a villein?" The boys looked surprised. "Aye, he is a freeman now, but his tas was born a villein. The miller's wife tells me that he aspires to be Sir John's steward of the manor after we return from France. That is why he follows the squire like a dog with his nose pressed into the cleft of that boy's buttocks."

\* \* \*

Hedyn leaned on his hoe and gazed west across Fowey Moor. The craggy peak of Brown Willy punctuated the featureless landscape four miles away. Hedyn had dreamed of someday climbing the hill, the highest peak in Cornwall. He was told that one could see all the way to the ocean from its heights. But it may as well have been a thousand miles away, for it was on a different manor, in a different parish. He could never leave Altarnon unless it pleased his master.

But now, Hedyn had no longing to climb Brown Willy. His desire to scale the great hill had been replaced by hazy dreams of going

31

to France as part of a great army. He would not only see the ocean, but he would sail upon it. He could scarcely believe it.

"Brown Willy will not grow wings and fly away, boy. You don't have to keep an eye on it," said Jago.

Hedyn smiled foolishly and returned to his work.

"Tas, Roger says that the boys in Sir John's company are to be paid a half penny a day."

"Roger will get his half penny; you will not."

"But Tas, why will I get no wages?"

"You are a villein. Your labor already belongs to Sir John. He does not pay you now does he? I receive no coin for being the ventenar, although Thomas Kelnystok will earn eight pence a day when his time comes."

Hedyn had been daydreaming about what he might buy with his money when he returned from France. "It's not fair! I too should get wages."

"Would you like for Sir John to leave you behind and take some other boy?"

Hedyn was silent for moment. He thought of how he had been treated by Squire John and the abuses that might be heaped upon him. He decided that he could endure the abuse for a chance to see some of the world.

"No, I've never set foot from this manor. I've never even seen a town. I don't want him to take some other boy. I want to go."

"And what of Squire John? Can you abide his mistreatment of you?" Jago asked.

Hedyn looked up at his father. "How did you know what I was thinking?"

"A tas knows his son's heart. I've seen the way he treats you. Chances are that he is simply full of himself and his new station. I pray that his cruel nature will not carry into manhood. Nevertheless, you will have to fend for yourself. I will not be there to offer what little protection I can give."

"I think I can abide Squire John. After all, he was once my friend," Hedyn said as he chopped a weed from the soft soil.

Jago stopped his work and turned to his son. "Hedyn, Sir John thinks well of you to have you serve his company." He leaned on his hoe. "But you must understand that this is a serious matter. You have heard Thomas and I tell stories of going to war for the last King Henry against Hotspur Percy. We tell only stories that make us laugh, or make us happy, or bring us pride. We tell no tales that bring us sadness. War is filth, toil, sickness, and death. Death can come swiftly from the blade, or a man can die slowly from the bloody flux. For a soldier, war starts with excitement and joy. But even with victory, war ends in grief."

Hedyn listened to his father, but he did not hear. He could imagine only banners, drummers, shining armor, and glory. But most of all, he longed to see what lay beyond Altarnon Parish.

# CHAPTER SIX

**Saint Nonna's Green**
**Altarnon Parish, Cornwall**
**6 August 1415**

"Yeeoow!" Hedyn jumped when the old horse nipped him on the rump. He turned quickly to swat the horse's nose away. She laid her ears back and glared at him with her one good eye. He rubbed his arm where the mare had bitten him earlier in the day. A big, black bruise shaped like the mare's teeth still throbbed under his tunic sleeve. He lengthened his hold on the horse's rope to allow him to stand farther away from her teeth.

Roger laughed, "Bite you again? You must remember to stay clear of her front and back. That beast kicks too!"

Hedyn sighed and rubbed his arm again. He peered around Roger and his horse to see farther up the lane. *What is taking so long? We should be moving by now.*

Sir John assembled his whole company along a narrow lane in the woods near Penpont. He planned a grand procession along the road past Saint Nonna's Church where the whole manor would see them off to war. Hedyn was amazed at how much space the company took up along the trail. There were five men-at-arms, each mounted on a large, sturdy war-horse, or courser as they called them. Two extra coursers for each man were also herded behind them. The twenty archers sat astride palfreys, which were small saddle horses, and a herd of twenty extra palfreys mingled with the extra coursers. The archers took turns minding the herd.

A large ox cart carried the pavilions, tents, food, cooking pots, extra armor, and extra weapons that every company required. Two of the archers' wives, who would cook and clean for the company, minded the cart and the oxen.

Father Stephen and his palfrey danced nervously in the middle of it all. He unfastened his sash and pulled his brown woolen robe up to his waist to be able to sit astride the saddle. Flashes of his pasty white legs, which rarely saw daylight, stood out against the horse's dark coat. He was no horseman, and he nervously eyed every other horse as if it meant to topple him from the saddle and trample him underfoot.

Last in the line were Hedyn and Roger. Their worn out palfreys were packed high with sacks of grain for the herd. Thomas Kelnystok promised the boys that they would be able to ride as soon as the grain was used up. It would be a two-day walk to Plymouth, where they would take shipping. From Plymouth they would sail to Southampton to meet King Henry's army.

"I still do not see why we were not given surcoats like the rest," Roger grumbled.

King Henry's army had no uniform. Each man wore what was within his own means. However, the king did require each knight to provide his retinue with simple white linen surcoats, with a crimson cross sewn onto the breast and back. The loose-fitting, sleeveless garments were worn over armor and other clothing. Henry hoped that the matching white surcoats would prevent the men from accidentally killing their friends during the heat of battle.

Hedyn wished he had a surcoat too as he watched the men waiting along the trail. The crisp white linen on the men-at-arms and archers seemed to gleam in the dappled sunshine that filtered through the trees.

Finally, the column of thirty people, fifty-eight horses, and four oxen began moving slowly from the woods and out onto Saint Nonna's Green. Hedyn heard people cheering long before he left the shade of the trees and led his mare into the bright August sun.

"People—so many people!" he said to Roger. Roger smiled over his shoulder in return. *All the people of Trewint, Treween, and Penpont must be here!* He had never seen so many folk in one place.

"Hedyn! Hedyn!" The boy's eyes were drawn to his sister and parents in the crowd that lined the road. Tressa jumped up and down and waved frantically. She wore the new kirtle that Guen had sewn for her. Where Jago found the money to buy the linen, he could not guess. For the first time, Hedyn realized that he would miss his little sister as much as he would miss his mother and father. Guen smiled, but her cheeks were wet with tears. Jago's pride showed on his face, but he wore no smile.

35

"*Duw genes*!" Jago shouted to Hedyn.

"God be with you too," Hedyn answered.

Hedyn suddenly felt his pride soar. For a moment he allowed himself to believe the cheers were for him alone and that he would return from France a great hero. He would become the greatest archer in all of Cornwall, perhaps in all England.

Hedyn's wispy daydream evaporated when the cheers turned to roaring laughter. He looked up just in time to see Father Stephen tumble from his nervous horse. The priest rolled backward off of the mount's rump. His feet went skyward and the hem of his robe dropped to cover his head and shoulders. He wore only a dirty linen shift underneath, which followed the robe over his head. The whole parish got a long look at the mortified priest's wide arse before he finished tumbling.

Denzel caught the skittish horse and held it as Stephen adjusted his robe and tried to regain his dignity as he remounted.

"Father, if you would wear a brais around your loins like the rest of us, you would not risk giving such a show!"

A man shouted out from the crowd, "Aye, that is a show we will all be struggling to un-see!"

The loud clatter of horses' hooves on the packhorse bridge deadened the last of the crowd's laughter. Hedyn, still bringing up the rear of the company, turned for one last glance of his family as he started to cross. He was disappointed that he could no longer see them in the crowd.

* * *

The August heat beat upon the company as they made their way along the road to Plymouth. Clouds of dust swirled up from feet and hooves. To Hedyn it seemed like an endless series of hills and valleys. He coughed constantly to clear the grit from his mouth and nose. Roger fared no better. At the rear of the column they ate everyone else's dust. The boys had been given nothing to drink since they left Penpont early that morning. Hedyn felt he would die of thirst.

They wound down a steep lane that opened into a beautiful green valley. The ox cart they followed began to slow.

36

"Looks like we are stopping!" Roger said with a cough. "They are stopping in that stream ahead!"

The whole company stood in a broad ford on the River Tamar. Hedyn's mare stuck her nose in the water as soon as she reached it. She seemed to inhale the water as she filled her belly. Hedyn fell to his knees, but before he could drink, William Whitwell rose above him astride his palfrey.

"Boys, drink none of this water!" he commanded.

Hedyn and Roger looked at him in astonishment.

"You may wash the dust from your face, but do not drink. This water will sicken you," he explained.

"But the horses drink!" Roger exclaimed.

"Aye, a horse can drink this, but a man cannot. The river drains from those fields yonder and carries sickness. While we are on this campaign, drink only ale or water from springs and wells, not from flowing streams."

Hedyn noticed that none of the other men were drinking.

"But William, why not streams? And why do the horses not get sick?" Hedyn asked.

"No one knows for sure, lad. The writings of Galen of Pergamon read that water drained from fields carries a miasma that upsets the balance of humours in the body, and . . . "

Whitwell suddenly looked apprehensive and stopped in mid-sentence. Roger splashed water on his face and paid no attention to the conversation.

"Never mind. Do not drink this water. Thomas tells me we will be stopping soon for ale and bread. Also, when you cross this river, you will leave Cornwall and be in Devonshire. We shall lodge in Tavistock tonight and arrive in Plymouth before the sun sets on the morrow."

Hedyn could not be sure, but he thought that William Whitwell just revealed that he could read. He knew no one else who could truly read except his priests. Even Sir John could barely write his own name. He wondered why William would try to conceal such an important skill.

The company stopped at a small hamlet on the Devonshire side of the river. A broom standing on end outside of a cottage door announced that the occupants had extra ale to sell.

Hedyn smacked his lips. The thick ale, heavy with the taste of grain, nourished him as well as slacked his thirst. Roger cupped his free hand under his big chunk of crumbling horse bread. Hedyn did not like the mixture of peas and barley meal in the bread but was grateful to have it just the same. The boys sat with their backs against the rough stones of the cottage wall. Hedyn took a big bite too. His hunger ignored the taste as he gobbled the coarse bread down. He stopped and looked into the clay jar that held his ale.

"Roger, remember what William said of drinking from the river? Folks make soup, pottage, and ale from streams that drain from fields. Why do those things not make us sick, but the ordinary water will?"

Roger drained the last drops from his jar, smacked his lips, and then burped a long, deep belch. "Hedyn, you are always wondering on the most fanciful notions."

A young man hurried past the pair with an armload of jars.

"Brewster, where do you draw water to brew your ale?" Hedyn asked.

The man stopped. "Why, from yon river. What is it to you?" he answered impatiently.

"How does water that will sicken not do so when it is made into ale?" Hedyn asked earnestly.

The young brewer snorted. "Because Saint Brigid, the patron saint of ale, changes it for us of course! Do you not know that she used to turn bathwater into ale?" The ale maker snorted again and hurried on.

Hedyn found no satisfaction with the answer but was too weary to think on it any longer. He burped, leaned his head against the wall, and tried to steal a few minutes of sleep before the company continued its march to the sea.

# CHAPTER SEVEN

**Plymouth Town**
**Devonshire, England**
**8 August 1415**

The company halted when a wide vista opened before them. Men left the column and moved to the forefront to join Sir John and the squire. Everyone, even Hedyn and Roger, moved so they could see the view.

The trek from Tavistock to Plymouth had been an easy one. A light rain had killed the dust and the Plymouth Road crossed only a few streams. The ox cart bogged down once but with the shoulders of twenty men pressed against it, the mud yielded quickly.

The walled town of Plymouth stretched southward before them. Two stone church towers protruded skyward from the clusters of simple one- and two-story shops and timber dwellings. Beyond the town wall to the southeast lay Sutton Pool, an inner harbor, where a score of single-masted cogs sat docked or anchored in the placid water. Beyond the town and Sutton Pool, Plymouth Sound opened to an endless sea that stretched to the horizon.

The view left Hedyn spellbound. He had never seen a true town. Such a collection of streets, buildings, and people fascinated him. A faint hum drifted to his ears. It took a moment for him to realize that it was the mingling of a thousand different sounds emanating from the town. The number of people coming and going in afternoon light convinced him that this must be the biggest city in England. The company rode down the hill and entered a gate into Plymouth. Even before Hedyn reached the town walls, his nose began to detect unpleasant hints of what lay ahead.

Hedyn was no stranger to bad smells. Pigsties, outhouses, and dung heaps all added to the aroma of farm life. But in the country, breezes carried away the bad smells and brought the fragrance of new mown hay, barley fields, and brewing ale. Here, the narrow streets and town walls did not allow even the sea breezes to carry away the stench of human waste, tanner shops, and slaughter pens. The fouled air of the town had a pervading sour smell of universal rot. A woman opened a window on the second story of a home and tossed the contents of a chamber pot onto the road in front of Hedyn. He flinched when he realized that the mud he trod upon was more than simple soil.

Hedyn's head spun with the shock to his nose. Most of the townsmen ignored the archers and men-at-arms as they made their way through the narrow lane past Saint Mary's church. Other people pushed and jostled to get through the men and horses of the company that clogged the road. The upper stories of many buildings were wider than the first floor and hung over the street. It made the street seem even narrower. Dogs trotted between the legs of the horses, and wandering pigs rooted through rubbish in alleys and side lanes. A group of children formed and trailed the company with palms up and extended. Hedyn barely understood their dialect of English, but he could see that they were begging for food or pennies.

"Pots mended! A penny to mend your pot!"

"Berries! A farthing for ripe berries!"

"Pasties! Pasties! Hot meat pasties!"

It seemed to Hedyn that all the merchants and street vendors cried their services and wares at the same time. Church bells, the clang of a blacksmith, and the squeal of pigs added to the clamor.

Hedyn had entered the town in wonder, but a new, uncomfortable feeling overcame him. The town seemed to be closing in around him. He felt as if he could not draw breath, and what breath he could gain was malodorous. He looked over to see a small boy peeing into the lane with his mother waiting patiently behind. Hedyn put down his head and trudged on, looking only at the hooves of Roger's horse before him. He wished that he could be outside the walls where the wind drifted and there were no jostling people, rooting hogs, or smell of decay.

The march through the town lasted only fifteen minutes, but it seemed much longer to Hedyn. He breathed a deep sigh of relief as they passed through the Barbican Gate out onto the quay of Sutton Pool. A softer odor of tar, seawater, and fish replaced the stink of the city streets.

"Christ's bones! That whole place stinks like a tord!" Roger still held his nose.

Roger's father came to check on his son. "Well, boys, what do you think of Plymouth Town?" His father asked with a grin.

"Tis not what I expected, Tas," Roger said. "The people seemed unfriendly. And the smell!"

"Ventenar, are all towns this way? It must be the greatest town in all Christendom!" added Hedyn.

"Nay, it is not so large as you might think. I hear that London Town is twenty times greater." He paused and laughed. "And stinks a hundred times more! Boys, we will wait here on the quay while Sir John finds our shipping. I'll soon be sending William Whitwell and the two of you back into town to buy bread and ale."

* * *

As the sun was setting behind the town walls, the boys pulled like oxen on a handcart loaded with rations. Whitwell led the way, and the crowd parted warily for the trio as they crossed the lane back to the Barbican Gate. A great cask of ale sat in the cart among stacks of oatcakes and dried codfish. The codfish had been cut open and flattened before salting and drying. They were hard and stiff and clattered like wood shingles when they were dumped in the cart.

Hedyn struggled with the cart through the mud and bumped into Whitwell. The big archer had stopped without warning. Suddenly, he darted through the crowd. He moved fast, head down, and vanished into an ally on the opposite side of the lane. He reappeared for a flash in the distance as he slipped back through the Barbican Gate to Sutton Pool. The boys watched him in astonishment.

The boys' eyes were still focused on the Barbican Gate, trying to catch sight of Whitwell, when a question startled them. Two monks emerged from the crowd and stood over them.

"Who have we here?" the older of the two monks asked. Neither of the boys responded, but instead looked at the monk in trepidation.

"Speak when the abbot addresses you," the younger monk added. He stood a full head taller that the older man.

"We…we are fetching food for Sir John's company. We are going to the wars in France," Hedyn finally offered.

41

"You are Cornish," the abbot said, noticing Hedyn's accented speech. The roly-poly abbot stood resting his hands on the top of his belly. His face remained passive, but Hedyn sensed something sinister in the abbot's eyes.

"Yeess," the abbot continued slowly with a hiss. "Sir John Trelawny of Altarnon, I have heard that he received an indenture from the king." He sniffed then added, "Pray tell, who was that tall man who left you here?" Neither boy answered.

"Speak, boys. Brother Andrew has asked you a question," the younger monk demanded. Hedyn remained cautious.

A sudden fear that he could not explain rose like bile in Hedyn's gut, and something told him that he should be careful of what he said. "Um, we know him not, Lord. He stopped and looked into our cart then hurried away," Hedyn answered quickly before Roger could respond. Hedyn did not know why he needed to lie to the abbot. But he knew that by Whitwell's sudden retreat, the archer did not want the monks to know that he was in Plymouth. Roger just looked at Hedyn and said nothing.

The abbot furrowed his brow and looked at the younger man. "I am sure that was he, Brother Ralph. I will send a report to Bishop Edmond in Exeter that we spied him here in Plymouth. We will seize that Lollard yet."

Brother Ralph turned to the boys and said, "Be on your way, boys, but if you see that man again before you sail, send word to the abbot. He will be visiting at the Lord Mayor's home."

Before they turned away, the abbot reached into the cart and took an oatcake. The boys watched as he tucked the cake under his arm and strolled away.

The boys struggled with the heavy cart back to the quay. Neither boy mentioned the theft of the bread.

"Hedyn, what is a Lollard?" Roger whispered.

"I know not. I have heard it said by the Father Leofric that Lollards must all be burned, but he did not say what they are," Hedyn answered. He stopped and leaned close to Roger.

"Let us not speak of this to the others, at least until we can discover if he is guilty of something. He has been kind to me, after all."

Roger thought for a moment then said, "Very well, if you think it best."

As the boys pulled the heavy cart through the gate and on to the quay, Hedyn hoped that he had done the right thing.

# CHAPTER EIGHT

**Plymouth Town**
**Devonshire, England**
**9 August 1415**

The horses boarded the ships after the weapons and food were secure on the decks. The archers tried to soothe them with soft talk and hands full of grain, but the sea frightened the beasts. The gangplank shifted with their weight, and bobbed slightly from the shallow swells in Sutton Pool. The horses eyed the plank nervously and struggled with each step, balking and tossing their heads

The ships seemed enormous to Hedyn. Thomas told the boys that the ships were called cogs, and they had been hired from Dutch captains to carry King Henry's army to France. Three cogs were dispatched to Plymouth to take on Sir John's company. Sir John, the men-at-arms, the cooks, and their archer husbands climbed aboard the newest and finest vessel. The remaining archers and all the livestock were divided between the other two ancient tubs. Father Stephen and the boys were assigned to an old cog that betrayed its age with many patches and repairs. It leaned lazily to one side in the water.

The ship was about eighty feet long with an open deck that normally held cargo bound between the ports of Europe. A raised deck over the bow and a similar raised deck over the stern provided small cabins for the Dutch crew. None of the Englishmen were invited to explore inside. They would remain on the open deck, exposed to the weather, for the entire voyage.

A long rowboat, tied off upside down, took up most of the space on the sterncastle. The sterncastle also held a horizontal wheel that the sailors pushed like a turnstile to swivel the rudder and turn the ship. From Plymouth Town they would follow the coast eastward to Southampton, where they would rendezvous with the king's army.

Crude stalls, made of simple, waist-high rails, would keep the horses for the voyage. Hedyn's palfrey may have settled down quickly, but she still eyed the boy with malice. Since she refused to eat from his hand without nipping his fingers, he placed a pile of grain on the deck where she could reach it.

Most of the men had never been aboard a ship. They were as excited as boys at a fair. Lawrence Woodstock, a broad-shouldered archer from Treween, hailed the Dutch captain of the cog.

"Master, does your ship have a name?"

"Ja. Haar naam is *Snelle Pijl*," the captain answered.

"*Snelle Pijl*? What does *Snelle Pijl* mean, master?" Lawrence asked.

"Swift Arrow. It means Swift Arrow," William answered before the captain could reply.

The archers stopped what they were doing and looked at one another in wonder. Arrows were central to their being and purpose. To them, the name of their ship could be no coincidence.

Father Stephen glanced from man to man then said, "Praise God! It is a good omen and a sign from the heavens! It heralds that King Henry will be successful and the men on this boat will be delivered safely home!" Half of the archers quickly made the sign of the cross.

There were smiles all around, and the archers murmured their approval with the priest's prediction. Hedyn noticed that William rolled his eyes, turned away, and busied himself with tying off his horses.

The voyage to Southampton would take three days and two nights. They could travel only as fast as the prevailing winds as they followed the coast eastward. *I can walk faster than this ship can sail*, Hedyn thought. Horses, men, and equipment crowded the open deck. Within the first day, both men and beasts became accustomed to the rolling deck and stood with wide stances to take the movement of the ship.

On the second night, a squall blew in from the British Sea and battered the cogs about like little twigs in a mill stream. The Dutch crewmen, accustomed to storms at sea, laughed at the cowering Englishmen. Horses squealed, and frightened archers emptied their seasick bellies into the fierce winds. Hedyn huddled with Roger and Thomas against the wall of the sterncastle. They braced themselves with each rise and crashing fall of the little ship. The rain blew sideways and stung their skin like a thousand watery needles. The heavens thundered,

45

and the flashes of lighting betrayed the fear on all the men's faces. None of the Altarnon men could even tread water, let alone swim.

Hedyn imagined that he would be tossed into the black water and sink beneath the waves. "Save us Saint Nonna and Saint David! Deliver us from this wind!" Hedyn prayed to his patron saints, but he was certain they could not hear him above the howling of the wind and crashing of the sea. Within an hour the storm passed, but the sea remained restless, and the pounding waves continued to torment the men. Hedyn and the Altarnon men had no sleep for the remainder of the night.

Dawn brought a smear of orange on the eastern horizon. The men were exhausted and bedraggled. The horses fared no better. They were as tired as if they had been ridden all night and stood with their heads hung low to the deck.

Hedyn stood looking over the rails. The growing light let him pick details from the dark shore. He could make out the other two cogs sailing ahead of them and felt relieved that they had not become separated during the storm. Hedyn's stomach heaved as a Dutch sailor next to him shoveled mushy peas into his mouth with gusto. He washed it down with cheap ale.

Hedyn turned to Roger. "I'll not break my fast. My belly will not take it this morning."

Roger looked pale. "Nor will I. None of the others can eat. None save for William."

Hedyn turned toward Whitwell and caught his eye. The rain had soaked the big archer, but he seemed less miserable than his mates. He pulled a piece of leather-like meat from a dried cod with his teeth. When he saw Hedyn looking at him, he smiled and lifted his fish in salute. Calling across the deck to the boys, he said, "Do not fret lads; the sickness will pass. You will get accustomed to the sea soon."

Hedyn gave a hesitant smile in return, then twisted and retched over the side. His empty belly surrendered nothing to the sea.

*  *  *

The waves grew calmer as the morning wore on. The sun had risen well above the horizon, when the Dutch sailors began gathering on the foredeck and pointing to the east. William joined them. He shielded his eyes from the sun and strained to see where they pointed. The other Englishmen soon gathered around.

William turned and explained to them, "That bump of land in the distance is the Isle of Wight. We shall pass in the strait to the north of the isle. That is called the Solent, and it will carry us to Southampton Water, where we will meet the king's army. We will be there before day's end."

The men nodded. Thomas asked, "You speak their tongue? Where did you learn?"

"I picked up a few words of Dutch in my travels." He offered no other explanation, but it seemed to satisfy Thomas.

The Isle of Wight sheltered the Solent from the waves of the British Sea. The cogs sailed through water as smooth as glass between the isle and the English mainland. Hedyn thought the deck looked like spring washday in his village. The sun and warm breeze offered a chance to dry rain-soaked clothing and equipment. Tunics, shirts, and hosen hung from railings and horse stalls. The men rubbed sheep tallow on swords and helmets to keep the rust away. Each man also had a dozen extra bowstrings laid out in the sun. A long bow could only give its full power if it had a perfectly dry hemp cord.

Hedyn and Roger stood on the foredeck and watched the cog in front of them slice through the water. The sun reflected from a million dazzling ripples in the ship's wake. Faint shouts and hoots drifted across the water from the lead ship and drew their attention far to the front. Soon the archers covered the foredeck of the *Snelle Pijl* and crowded around the boys.

"By all the saints! There is Henry's army!" cried Thomas Kelnystok.

Miles to their front, Hedyn could make out hundreds of white tents and marquis decorating the green shore.

"Look at the fleet!" another man added.

"Hedyn and Roger stood on the foredeck and watched the cog in front of them slice through the water."

Hedyn could see no fleet in the distance, but his eyes could make out what looked like a flooded forest at the end of the Solent. As his eyes adjusted to the bright sun, he realized that what he had perceived as trees growing from the water were masts. Fifteen hundred cogs and ships lay anchored in Southampton Water, ready to embark King Henry's army. Their masts rose up to form a man-made forest with yardarms for branches and canvas for leaves.

In another hour the three cogs were among the fleet and had dropped their anchor in shallow water. The men on the *Snelle Pijl* watched as sailors lowered a small rowboat over the side of Sir John's vessel. Sir John clambered aboard with four oarsmen. Before he rowed away, he stood and cupped his hand around his mouth.

"Wait here until I return," Sir John shouted to Thomas aboard the *Snelle Pijl*. Thomas raised his hand to show that he understood. He turned to his archers with his hands on his hips. "I wonder where he feared that we would wander." The men laughed excitedly.

"Sir John will be seeking the king's proctor to report that we have arrived. We will soon go ashore to wait for the army's departure. Repack your belongings and be ready. We shall take our leave from this rotten tub soon!"

The men cheered and the horses raised their heads and perked their ears as they sensed the excitement. Hedyn felt relieved that he would finally feel firm ground beneath his feet again.

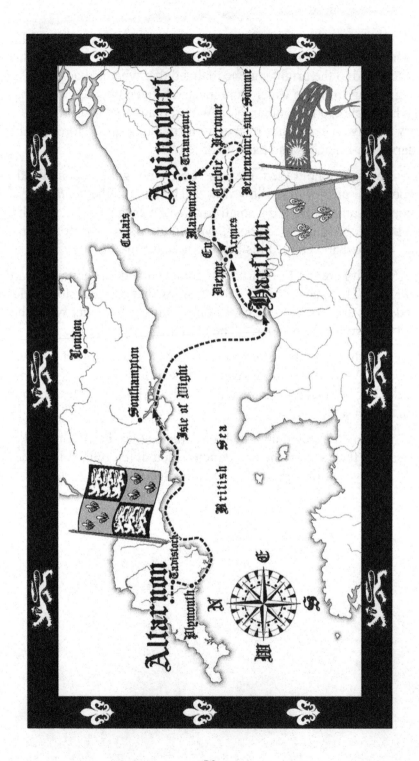

# CHAPTER NINE

## Southampton Water
## Hampshire, England
## 11 August 1415

"We have arrived too late to disembark, lads. We sail again on the morrow's ebb tide," Sir John called from his rowboat as it neared the *Snelle Pijl*. A groan rose up in unison from the throats of ten men and two boys. He added, "We shall stay afloat in preparation for the fleet's departure."

He turned to the men at the oars and said, "Row on," so that he could carry the news to the other ships. The sailors dipped their oars into the salty water and pulled.

The archers turned and threw their bundles to the deck. Although the Dutch sailors could not understand the words, they instantly knew there would be no leave on shore. Kicking the gunwales, they busied themselves settling the cog for the night.

"You heard Sir John. Find some space on the deck again and look after the horses," Thomas told his archers.

"How much longer must we endure this tub, Ventenar?" Lawrence Woodstock asked. Thomas only shrugged because he did not know. The man turned to William. "William of Devon, you seem to know a bit about sailing. How far must we go?"

The question startled William from his thoughts. The men rarely spoke to him, much less asked his opinion on any matter.

"The king has not announced the exact location in France. If God grants fair weather, it will take two days to cross the British Sea to Normandy. Five days if he takes us to Aquitaine."

"Aye. Let us hope that God and the Saints do grant fair weather," Lawrence said. The men sped up their efforts to prepare for the evening before them with the little light remaining.

Most of the men slept hard, catching up on the sleep they had lost to the storm the night before. Hedyn slept fitfully. He had never heard such snoring. The exhausted men seemed to be competing in volume, style, and duration.

51

The cloud-shrouded moon offered very little light, but Hedyn saw that Roger had curled up like a babe under his father's arm to sleep. Hedyn suddenly wished that his tas or mamm were here. For the first time he felt alone, and the distance from his home in Altarnon seemed immense. The excitement of travel and the newness of what he saw had kept his mind occupied. Now he wished his own father's snores bellowed from the darkness. He longed to be safely curled on his mat in his tiny cottage. He was thankful that the night concealed his silent tears.

Shuffling on the deck brought Hedyn out of his melancholy. He could just make out William Whitwell standing across the deck from him looking out over the anchored fleet. Hedyn rose, wiped his face on the back of his sleeve, and picked his way through snoring men. As he neared, he realized that William was in prayer, with his head bowed and his eyes closed. Hedyn stood silently beside him. William finished, crossed himself, and opened his eyes. He was startled to find Hedyn standing at his side.

"Oh, Hedyn! No sleep for you either?" the archer whispered.

"Only a deaf man can sleep with this crew," the boy answered.

"Ha, you are true," William said.

"William, for what do you pray?" Hedyn asked.

William thought for a moment then answered, "I pray for the safety of these men around me, for you, and for Roger. I pray that I may remain a good servant of my Lord."

"To what saint do you pray?" the boy asked.

The boy detected a faint smile on the big man's face in the dim light. "I pray to my God and Jesus Christ himself. I pray to no saint! Why, who do you pray to, young Hedyn?"

William's response puzzled the boy. "I pray to Saint Nonna, of course. She is the patron saint of Altarnon! Do you not send prayers to your favorite saint?"

"All saints are just men and women who have gone to heaven. They are not divine and cannot answer your prayers. The Holy Scriptures say: 'For there is one God and one mediator between God and men, Christ Jesus.' Do as the scriptures command and send your prayers to the blessed Jesus Christ. He is where your salvation lay."

Hedyn had never heard such a thing. Everyone prayed to saints - patron saints of places or work or maladies. The saints could speak directly to God on one's behalf. In addition to Saint Nonna, his father often prayed to Saint Josse to ensure a good harvest. When her children cut or bruised themselves, his mamm would pray to Saint Radegunde, the patron saint of sores and scabs. Praying directly to God seemed disrespectful. If folks needed prayer to Jesus, they would give a silver penny to a priest or a monk to pray for them. Everyone knew that God and Christ heard the prayers of saints and priests much clearer than ordinary people.

William looked around to ensure that no one listened. "I must thank you, Lad. You did not betray me to the monks in Plymouth Town. I am indebted to you for that."

"We told them that we did not know you." Hedyn leaned toward him and whispered. "That fat abbot said that you are a Lollard."

"I expect that he did," William whispered in response.

Hedyn waited for some explanation, but none came. Before he could ask any more questions about the abbot, William changed the subject.

"Where is your new bow?" the big archer asked.

"Packed with my other belongings," Hedyn answered.

"I want you to start wearing the bow, in its case, on your back. Wear it at all times, except when hard work makes it awkward. You will become an archer, and the bow should become part of you. Have you noticed that the men carry their bow always, and when it is not on their person it is in ready reach?" He paused and looked down at Hedyn.

"Aye, now that you make mention, they do always have their bows at hand," Hedyn said.

"Good. When you leave this pile of rotting timber and step on French soil, have your bow on your back or in your hand. It may save your life someday."

Hedyn nodded but could not tell if the big archer saw him in the dim starlight. "I will do as you say." Hedyn made the promise but wondered how the bow might save his life. He could barely string it much less draw it to his ear.

"Good." William replied. "I will try to sleep again despite this chorus of snores. You should do the same."

* * *

The bright August dawn found the fleet at Southampton buzzing with activity. Swarms of rowboats carried men and equipment between the bigger ships. The men on the *Snelle Pijl* waited impatiently for the tide to change. In mid-afternoon, an enormous ship with three masts emerged from the vast fleet. Its brightly painted forecastle and sterncastle shone in the bright sun. The top sails caught the morning breeze and moved her slowly to the open sea.

"Look yonder!" One of the men shouted and jabbed the air with his finger.

"That must be the *Trinity Royal*, King Henry's ship," William shouted above the excited clamor of the men. Just then, the great sail of the main mast unfurled, revealing the king's coat of arms painted on the canvas.

"Aye, it is the king indeed!" Father Stephen said.

The archers watched in wonder as the fleet came to life. Hundreds of sails unfurled to fill with wind and follow the *Trinity Royal* into the British Sea. The Dutchmen pulled in the anchor. Several sailors climbed up the lines, as nimble as monkeys, to unfurl the large single sail of the *Snelle Pijl*.

Shouts from their land side drew attention to smoke rising from one of the large ships. Hedyn could see men jumping from the gunwales into the water. Small boats began to pluck them from the sea. Within a few minutes the entire ship blazed fiercely, as savage tongues of flame licked up at the rigging. Wood, tar, and canvas made ships a tinder box, at mercy to the slightest spark.

"That is the Devil's own ship now," Father Stephen said as he made the sign of the cross. Several of the men followed his example.

While Hedyn hoped that all the men and boys got off the floating inferno, muted screams floating across the water told him that not all made it to safety. The men became subdued. The *Snelle Pijl* was a cheerless vessel as it moved slowly away, the smoldering ship at her stern. Hedyn thought that such a loss was surely a bad omen. The black pillar of smoke rose like a tower into the summer air. He watched until it disappeared behind the western horizon.

# PART TWO
## The Siege of Harfleur

Our King went forth to Normandy,
with grace and might of chivalry,
There God for him wrought marv'lously,
Wherefore Englond may call and cry,
To God give thanks O Englond, for the victory,
To God give thanks O Englond, for the victory,
He set a siege, forsooth to say,
To Harflur town with royal array,
That town he won and made the affray,
That France shall rue till Domesday:
To God give thanks.
The Agincourt Carol, c.1420

# CHAPTER TEN

## Mouth of the River Seine
## Normandy, France
## 13 August 1415

"It must be Normandy then. If we were going to Aquitaine, we would not spy land for at least two more days," Thomas Kelnystok said with confidence. He knew this because William had told him a few minutes before.

A broad inlet, formed by the mouth of a large river, spread into view. White chalk cliffs framed the inlet and rocky beach where they were to land. The afternoon sun, blazing from behind, caused the cliffs to gleam like snow.

"That must be the River Seine. If it was the Somme, I would recognize this place," William explained. "Only the Seine could be this big. And if it is the Seine, then we are in Normandy and we are surely to take Harfleur."

"Harfleur?" the men said almost in unison. All the men knew of Harfleur. Even Hedyn had heard of the Norman town of Harfleur.

"There will be many French crossbowmen waiting for us on those town walls," Thomas added.

"Aye, Thomas speaks true. Do you remember hearing of the great French raid on Plymouth Town a few years ago?" William asked the men. They nodded. "That raid, and many other raids on the English and Cornish coast, came from Harfleur. Henry will capture this town in revenge, and the port will offer him a fortified base for supplies." Under his breath, William added, "If we survive taking it."

The fleet neared the shore, and a brightly colored banner appeared on the high mast of the *Trinity Royal*. King Henry summoned his commanders to a council of war. Scores of rowboats slid through the water like ducklings to gather at their enormous mother hen.

The western sun sat on the watery horizon when the council ended and the commanders took off for their anchored ships. Sir John's rowboat bumped against the side of the *Snelle Pijl*, and the archers helped him climb aboard. The men bowed to their lord as he stepped down to the deck to relay the king's commands.

Sir John smiled at his men. "I trust all is in readiness to disembark on the morrow, Ventenar?"

"Aye, Sir John, we are all eager to get off this boat!" Thomas answered.

The men nodded their agreement.

"The whole army shares your wish." Chuckling, Sir John stepped up on the forecastle to be better seen and heard. "King Henry has given us orders which I will convey to you now." The men crowded in, forcing Roger and Hedyn, who were behind them, to stand on tiptoe.

"No man will go ashore without permission of the king, on pain of death.

No man will steal from or deface a church, on pain of death.

No man will kill a priest or monk unless attacked by said priest or monk, on pain of death.

No man will abuse any woman, on pain of death.

No man will cry havoc or plunder citizens loyal to King Henry ..."

"On pain of death," the men answered in unison.

Sir John laughed. "I think you understand, lads. This is to be a Christian campaign. Henry views the folk here as misguided subjects, not foreign enemies. He wants to welcome them back into the fold of his kingdom. Hence, no plundering."

"No plundering!?" Denzel grumbled and tugged at his beard. "How are we to make our fortunes?"

Thomas changed the subject. "Is it to be Harfleur, Sir John?"

"Aye, our first task is to take Harfleur. It lies on the Seine a few miles upriver," Sir John replied soberly.

The men grew somber.

"But first we must unload these ships on yonder shore. The French will not let us do so in peace. Their knights will be upon us on the morrow."

But no French knights met them with the morning sun. Nor did any appear on the second and third day. Each man and boy worked feverishly through three backbreaking days, ever wary of an imminent attack. The men rowed every weapon, every cooking pot, and every scrap of food to shore in small boats. They piled everything neatly on the beach above the high tide line where it could be repacked for the march inland.

Hedyn watched from afar while scores of men struggled to pull a great object up the beach. To Hedyn it looked like a massive iron tree trunk lashed with ropes to a giant wooden block. Roger halted his work to watch as well; both boys gazed in wonder.

"It is a gonne, boys. It can hurl a stone the weight of a man farther than the best archer can shoot an arrow," William explained.

The boys looked at him dumbly, as if he had spun some unbelievable yarn. They looked again. The men inched the cannon farther up the shore. The big archer laughed.

"Just you wait; when you hear a great clap of thunder and the sky is cloudless, you will know the gonne is doing its murderous business."

Squire John and Jan Tregeagle approached the working men, their boots crunching the gravel underfoot. "King Henry has sent a force inland to protect the landing," the Squire explained. The sea breeze tossed his hair and he pushed a strand out of his eyes. "But they have seen no French men-at-arms, only villeins fleeing their homes."

"I would wager my bow fingers that they are laying a trap!" Lawrence Woodstock exclaimed. He was the quietest man in Sir John's company. When he did speak, men listened. The men stopped to hear the squire's response.

The comment caught the squire off guard. "I...I had not considered such. Surely the force that the king sent inland would discover such treachery!"

"There is no trap." The archers turned at William's voice. "The French would never plan such a subtle scheme. They all fight

59

headstrong, impulsively, without regard to planning. Each knight and man-at-arms is out for his own glory. That is why they can often be beaten so easily."

"You are just a lowly archer. What gives the likes of you such confidence to know what the French might do?" Jan Tregeagle snarled. Tregeagle still held William in contempt for embarrassing him on the practice field.

"Because I've fought them before. I was here with the Duke of Clarence, the king's brother, when he came to the aid of the Burgundians three years ago."

The Altarnon men silently absorbed this revelation. Hedyn now understood why William knew so much about fighting, the sea, and Normandy. Squire John's eyes grew wide with new respect for William. Few men in Sir John's company had ever seen combat, and only William Whitwell had ever faced the French.

Ships crowded the inlet, each sending its cargo ashore in small boats. Companies of men from all over England toiled on the shore. The tide went out and the Dutchmen sailed the shallow draft cogs toward shore until their bows grounded and came to a stop on the gravel bottom. Pandemonium ensued when the sailors crowded the horses off the decks in a flurry of flailing hooves and frantic squeals. Each animal made a great splash of water. The horses struggled to right themselves and began the hundred-yard swim to the beach.

Hedyn watched in amusement until he noticed that one of the palfreys had injured itself in the fall. It could not keep its head above the water. The pitiful squeals and snorts horrified him as the horse disappeared for the last time beneath the waves. Hedyn shielded his eyes from the sun and struggled to see which horse had succumbed to a watery death. Had it been his ill-tempered mare? Disappointment flashed though Hedyn's mind when he spotted his horse stumbling up the rocky beach and shaking the seawater from her coat. It had been someone else's horse that had been lost after all. The old palfrey glared at Hedyn, insulted by the whole affair.

Hedyn cautiously approached and grasped her bridle. The mare turned to him, flared her nostrils, and took in his familiar scent. He placed his hand on her dripping neck and felt the muscles relax under his touch. For the first time, she allowed him to stroke her neck and scratch her ears. Instead of biting, she nuzzled his back as he led her placidly off the beach. This surprised him, and he felt a bit guilty for hoping she had not survived her swim to shore.

# CHAPTER ELEVEN

**The Siege lines of Harfleur**
**Normandy, France**
**25 August 1415**

"Wait, I've lost me boot again!" Roger called out.

King Henry's army lived in a sea of mud created by the defenders of Harfleur. They had flooded the ground around the walled town to keep the English away. The water had receded, but the soil remained wet and sticky. A light wind brought the stench of moldy decay from the marshes.

Hedyn stopped and turned. The mud had sucked Roger's boot off his foot three times this day. "Hurry, Roger! Your tas says he must have more arrows now. Roger pulled his boot from the mud and slipped it back on his foot. He lost his balance and sat down heavily. Hedyn knelt and tied the boot for him.

"What is wrong with you, Roger? You have grown slow and clumsy in the last few days," Hedyn asked.

Roger tried to smile as Hedyn helped him to his feet. "Just a bit weary."

The siege of Harfleur was ten days old. Hedyn and Roger toiled each day, all day, to supply Sir John's men on the front lines. They carried food, drink, and arrows from the baggage train, past the latrines and offal pits, through the camps, and across the muddy gray landscape to where the Altarnon men worked and fought.

The archers dug trenches and built parapets to protect themselves and the large cannon that bombarded Harfleur. They dug at night and dodged French crossbows during daylight. Every few days, they rested in the camps while another company took their place on the front lines.

Henry divided his army in two parts. The king's brother, the Duke of Clarence, commanded half the men and entrenched on the east side of Harfleur. That division guarded the road to Rouen and Paris from where French reinforcements might come. King Henry's division besieged the town from the west. Both halves of the army operated on the only strips of elevated ground. The stinking marshes, which swelled with the tides, surrounded the army to the north and south.

The walls of Harfleur filled Hedyn with awe when he first saw them ten days before. The stone walls were three times higher than a man and stretched over two miles around the town. From the twenty-six tall towers along the wall, crossbowmen could see and shoot at anyone who approached. A small harbor, connected by a channel to the river, also lay within the walls. Three gates entered the town, each protected by stout defensive barbicans. The barbicans were a separate fortification with double towers and battlements that protected each gate from the front and sides. The Montivilliers Gate and Rouen Gate were also protected by deep moats and were unassailable. King Henry's only chance to smash his way into Harfleur lay at the Leure Gate, on the western side. Its massive timber and earth barbican towered in front of the English trenches and the moats were narrower and shallower there.

The boys reached the baggage train and found a score of carts that had just arrived from England. Canvas sheets covered high stacks of arrow sheaves in each cart. A tall, lanky man stood by the first cart. He asked through a snaggletoothed grin, "Be it arrows you seek, lads?" He lifted up the corner of a canvas cover and began pulling sheaves from the pile. Hedyn knew that each bundle contained twenty-four arrows, but he could not begin to count how many sheaves were in each cart.

The number of arrows astonished Hedyn. He never imagined this many arrows could be made so quickly for the war. "How many are here?" Hedyn asked in astonishment.

"I reckon there are about a hundred thousand here—and more to come. The fletchers and arrowsmiths have been busy back home," Snaggletooth Man said.

"How did they find enough feathers?" Hedyn asked as he peeked under the canvas.

"Did you not hear? King Henry commanded his sheriffs to collect six feathers from every goose in their shires, three from the right wing and three from the left. Every goose in England has done its part for the war!" the man said with a laugh.

Roger stared at the man's hand when he held out a sheave of arrows. The first two fingers of his right hand were gone. Snaggletooth

Man held up his mangled hand. "Is it this you see, lad?" The boys looked at the man with wide eyes.

"Let this be a lesson to you, lads. They was chopped off by a French knight. The Frenchies hate English archers more than the devil his self. I got myself caught by the French three year ago when I fought with Duke Clarence. The saints protected me, and I got away before they slit my gullet.

"They cut off your bow fingers!" Hedyn exclaimed.

"Aye, I'll never pull a bow cord again, but I can bring arrows to those who do," the man said through a toothless grin. "Do not get captured by the French and you will keep your bow fingers and your life. Now lads, I'll load you up with arrows to take to your archers. I want these sticking in some Frenchman's arse before this day ends."

The boys bent under the weight of their loads. Each had seven sheaves, 168 arrows, wrapped in a coarse cloth and strapped to their backs. Roger began to fall behind as they trudged forward to the front lines. He slowed, then stopped.

"Wait; I cannot keep pace," Roger cried out in frustration.

Hedyn turned clumsily with his load. "Roger, you are larger and stronger than I. Why can you not keep up?" Roger's slowness irritated Hedyn, until he saw the desperation in the boy's face. He felt guilty for chiding his friend.

"Here, I shall take part of your load." Hedyn removed two sheaves of arrows from Roger's pack and put them into his own. "That should help. Roger, you lead the way and set the pace." Hedyn shifted his bow case to one side and re-shouldered the enlarged bundle. He grunted as he felt the full load.

Roger started again with new vigor, but he quickly began to slow. He stumbled and fell to his hands and knees. His bundle of sheaves scattered across the ground.

Hedyn dropped his load. He knelt by his friend and helped him turn to sit up.

"Roger, are you un-well?" Hedyn asked.

"I am only weary from the heat!" Roger insisted.

Roger grimaced in pain and held his hands across his belly as a massive cramp twisted his insides.

"Roger, this is more than weariness. Tell me what is wrong!" Hedyn demanded.

"I have a griping in my guts. My innards seem to squeeze and twist. It has grown worse. I have gone to the latrine half-score times this day already. Nothing comes out but brown water."

"Why did you not tell me?" Hedyn asked softly.

"It would serve no end. We have too much to do," Roger answered. Roger bent double as a painful cramp tightened his insides.

Hedyn helped him to his feet. Roger stood and wobbled. His eyelids fluttered, and he crashed back to the earth in a dead faint.

"Roger! Roger!" Hedyn yelled frantically. He shook his friend but got no response. Other men and boys passed them going to the camps or returning to the front. Most just stepped around and ignored the lifeless boy who lay in the mud.

"Please, someone help us! My friend is ill!"

Most men just shook their heads at him and hurried past. Finally, an old white-haired knight with a fatherly look stopped. He took off his battered old helmet and held it under his arm.

"Does he have the camp disease?" the old knight asked.

"I know not, sire. He said that he has a griping in his guts. He fainted and I cannot wake him!"

"Just as I feared. With this heat and damp, the bloody flux will be upon this army. Your friend is not the first. I have heard that the Bishop of Norwich also has the flux. There will be many more, I wager. See if you can get him up, and I will hail a cart for him. To whose company do you belong?"

"They belong to my father's company." Hedyn looked up to see Squire John approaching.

"Thank you, good sir, for your assistance. I will take charge of these two waywards now. My father sent me to discover what has delayed them. He needs those arrows," Squire John said with an air of self-importance.

"Wayward indeed! Over-worked boys if you ask me. Take heed, young squire. Your servants can only take care of you if you take care of them." The old knight slid his helmet back on his gray head and continued down the path.

Squire John looked down on the boys with scorn. "I will commandeer a cart and take him to camp." The squire turned and walked to the closest cart that trundled along the path. Hedyn could see him talking to the carter. Roger opened his eyes slowly when Hedyn began to move him.

"We shall get you to camp where you can rest," Hedyn told him.

"I should not have drunk from the river that goes by camp. William Whitwell warned us, but the ale was so sour that day. I could not take it, so I drank from the river. I am sorry. . ." Roger's eyes filled with tears.

The ox cart stopped in front of the boys, and the carter helped Hedyn lift Roger into the bed of the cart. "I am sorry, Hedyn," Roger repeated.

"You have no cause to be sorry," Hedyn answered and he began to climb up next to him.

"No, villein's son. You have arrows on the side of the path that are needed by my archers. You must deliver them before you tend Roger. I shall see that the carter takes Roger to camp."

"But, Squire!" Hedyn protested.

"Go! Now!" Squire John commanded and pointed down the path to the front line.

Roger turned on his side so he could see his friend. "Go, Hedyn. Take the arrows and tell my tas."

Before Hedyn could turn away, Roger whispered through a mirthless smile, "And keep your bow fingers."

# CHAPTER TWELVE

**The Siege lines of Harfleur**
**Normandy, France**
**26 August 1415**

Ka-boooom!

A thunder-like crash echoed across the salt marsh and off the stone walls of Harfleur. The Altarnon men looked toward the cloudless sky and smiled at each other sheepishly.

"The gonne has fooled me again," Sir John laughed. "I look at the sky for rain each time it fires!"

Hedyn watched as the cannon stone struck the Leure Gate barbican in a spray of dust and splinters. Several logs collapsed and a river of rocks and dirt cascaded from the breech. A cheer went up from the English lines.

For just a moment, Hedyn was distracted from his worry about Roger. After delivering the arrows to the front line, he was not allowed to return to camp to tend to him. Sir John and the squire found too many duties for him. "We need you here, lad. Thomas will be allowed to go attend to his son," Sir John explained to him. When informed of his son's illness, Thomas had hurried to join Roger.

\* \* \*

King Henry brought twelve cannons for the siege. The gunners named the cannon near Hedyn's part of the line "The King's Daughter." She was fired three times a day; the complicated loading of the heavy projectiles allowed nothing faster. The first time it fired, Hedyn pressed his palms over his ears and fell to the ground. The ungodly blasting of the air and sulfurous stench from the clouds of smoke led Father Stephen to declare that the great gun was the work of the devil. Even after Hedyn grew to expect it, he still jumped at the noise.

"We took a big chink from the gate that time!" Squire John said as he shielded his eyes from the sun and looked at the gate.

"Aye, but they will patch it during the night," William responded.

"Look sharp, Sire! They always answer with their crossbows when the gonne fires," William reminded Sir John. He and the other men-at-arms dropped the visors on their helmets and squatted in the trench to provide less of a target. As if on cue, the French crossbowmen poured a shower of short, fat arrows at the English lines. Some of the quarrels, as the short crossbow arrows were called, sailed over the men's heads. Others fell short. None made their mark.

They were about two hundred and fifty paces from the walls of Harfleur, just inside longbow range. The French crossbows could shoot farther, but lacked the accuracy of the longbow. A crossbow was also slow to reload. An English archer could get off several arrows for each French quarrel.

After the first hail of quarrels, the archers came to their feet and loosed five or six arrows each at the Frenchmen on top of the walls. Hedyn thought he heard a distant yelp, and someone shouted "*Blasphémateurs*" He imagined a Frenchman with an arrow in his rump, just as Snaggletooth Man had hoped.

"Back down, lads. They have had time to reload," William shouted out.

All the men crouched except Lawrence of Woodstock. "Me bowstring snapped. I'll just change it out."

Hedyn sat on the floor of the trench near the broad-shouldered archer. "Lawrence, please get down. You know they will shoot again."

"They ain't hit none of us yet, lad," Lawrence replied just as a quarrel stabbed into the dirt in front of the trench. He looked up, just as another quarrel pierced his right eye and passed through his brain. The heavy iron point came out the back of his head and lodged in his helmet from the inside. The impact knocked him off his feet and tossed him to the rear of the trench, where he slid down into a sitting position. Hedyn sat and watched in horror at Lawrence's twitching body.

A hundred French voices cheered and taunted from the town walls.

Sir John screamed in rage and hurled profanities at Harfleur that Hedyn had never heard before. "Shoot, shoot," he screamed.

The Altarnon men jumped to their feet and began loosing arrows at a frantic pace. The shower of deadly missiles chased the French from the parapets and silenced the cheers.

"Hold your arrows, lads. There are none left to shoot at," William called out.

Hedyn sat and watched the last bit of life flow from Lawrence's body. He had never seen a man killed before. Lawrence's chest heaved one last time, and then he was still. Several of the archers crawled to where the body lay, suddenly afraid to expose themselves above the rim of the trench.

"He were a good man, he was," Denzel said.

"Aye, and left a good woman and two little 'uns back home. Who will care for them now?" another archer added. They pulled him down and laid him on his back. Denzel tried to extract the quarrel, but it was wedged too tightly into the steel of the helmet. He turned and said, "I can't get the helmet off, Sir John. It is pinned to poor Lawrence's head."

"It will go with him to his grave," Sir John said with sorrow. "When night falls, we shall bring a cart forward and take him to the burying ground."

The burying ground. Hedyn hadn't thought about a burying ground. It had not occurred to him that a place to bury the English dead would even be needed.

"William, why do the French call us that name?" Hedyn asked.

William looked at him. "Name? What name, boy?"

"*Blasphémateurs*. I hear the French yell that at us from the wall, all the time," said Hedyn.

"Oh. Yes, I see. It is blasphemers in English. The Frenchmen hear our foul-mouth soldiers take the Lord's name in vain constantly, so they consider all English to be blasphemous. They think we are all damned and going to the Devil." William answered.

Hedyn wondered if he was damned, if the whole of Henry's army was damned. They had come across the British Sea to wage war. But

69

now, as he avoided looking into Lawrence of Woodstock's dead face, he could not remember why.

"Hedyn, come hither," Squire John commanded. Hedyn tried not to look at Lawrence as he crawled past his body, but he could not help stealing a glance. The head lay awkwardly to one side with the fletching of the quarrel protruding from one eye socket. His other eye was open but looked sleepy and unconcerned about the fate of its owner.

"We shall sit tight until night fall," Squire John said. "I'll not risk moving Lawrence while the French can see and shoot. You shall go with him and ensure that he is properly buried. Then you may go and inquire about Roger. Thomas is to return to his duties here."

Hedyn nodded and looked at the sun. It would be hours before he could leave the trench.

*  *  *

Hedyn felt every bump on the trail as he sat next to Lawrence in the cart. The ground had finally dried in the August heat, and the mud had yielded to dust. Lawrence's good eye looked at him sleepily in the bright moonlight. Hedyn moved to the other side so he could not see the dead archer's face.

The cart slowed and then stopped. "This is the burying ground. You and your friend will be gettin' off here," the carter said over his shoulder.

Before Hedyn could move, two men appeared from the dark. One was Snaggletooth Man. "One of these is still kicking. I guess we will leave him be," Snaggletooth Man laughed.

"You gave me arrows yesterday and told me to keep my bow fingers," Hedyn said in surprise.

"Aye, I reckon I did. I carted arrows yesterday, and this day my business is burying dead 'uns. Business is lively—very lively, I must say," Snaggletooth Man replied.

"Have that many men been killed?" Hedyn asked.

"Some killed. Most of me customers are croakin' from the bloody flux. Business is lively."

70

Hedyn looked over the side of the cart. A score of bodies lay in a row on the side of the trail waiting for burial. Snaggletooth Man and his companion pulled Lawrence feet first out of the back of the cart and onto his feet. The body had stiffened in rigor mortis. For a moment, Lawrence seemed to stand on his own accord before he was lowered to the edge of the trail and laid beside his dead comrades. Hedyn shuddered. He jumped from the cart and ran from the burying ground as fast as his feet could carry him.

The moonlight cast eerie shadows from the trees and tents as he picked his way through the army's camps. At last, Hedyn found Sir John's pavilion with Father Stephen sitting under a canvas fly at its entrance. He stopped in front of the priest and tried to catch his breath.

"Son of Jago, you look as though you have seen a spirit!"

"Lawrence of Woodstock is killed. Sir John wishes Thomas to return to the trenches," Hedyn finally said.

"Come, sit down and rest. I will get you some pottage and ale," Father Stephen said. "But I'm afraid that Thomas can offer nothing to Sir John now. He did not take it well, you see. And I think he also may have the camp disease."

Hedyn shook his head as he sat on a camp stool. "Did not take it well? I don't understand you."

"His boy dying and all. Oh! You did not know. Poor Roger died late in the day." The priest held out a cup of ale, but Hedyn did not take it.

Hedyn looked at the priest dumbly. His mind could not digest what his ears told him.

"You and Roger were friends, were you not? I am sorry for you."

Hedyn could find no words, so the priest went on. "He got worse when he was brought here yesterday morn. He could not keep down the food or ale. It made him throw up, so I gave him some water. He only got sicker. His illness turned to the bloody flux."

Hedyn finally spoke. "From where did you draw water? Roger said the water made him sick."

Father Stephen became defensive. "I got it from yon river, but I prayed to Saint Arnold to bless it and make it pure."

"Where is he? Where is Roger now?" Hedyn asked sharply.

"He was taken away before dark to the burying ground." Before Father Stephen finished his sentence, Hedyn was on his feet and running back from where he came.

"But, your ale!" Father Stephen held up the cup as the boy melted back into the night.

* * *

The burying ground was not a graveyard where each man rested separately with a headstone to keep his memory. Instead, it was a long trench just wide enough for the length of a man and deep enough so the winter rains could not wash out the bones. Men were laid side-by-side down the trench and covered as they were placed. Once the soil concealed their faces, the men would forever be known only to God.

Half a dozen men dug with picks and spades to lengthen the trench; another six moved dead men into the trench and covered them with the loose earth. Hedyn was frantic by the time he reached the burying ground.

"My friend! My friend!" was all that Hedyn could say through his tears as he scurried from body to body peering into moonlit faces. Roger was not among them. The gravediggers stopped working for a moment and looked his way, then continued their gruesome task.

Snaggletooth Man appeared in a shaft of moonlight. "What's this? Were you not here earlier delivering a dead 'un?" he asked.

"I, I cannot find my friend. Have you seen a boy?" Hedyn could not bring himself to say *dead boy*. "My friend was brought here, and I cannot find him."

Snaggletooth Man scratched his balding head. "Aye, there was a boy this day, just before dark. It always pains me to see the young 'uns. Come with me."

Hedyn followed the man up the trench, stumbling over dirt clods in the dark. He realized they were walking over newly buried men, maybe even Lawrence of Woodstock.

"I reckon the boy would be somewheres about here." The man swept his arm in a wide arc over the mass grave. He turned and left Hedyn standing alone in the dark.

Hedyn fell to his knees in the loose soil. "Roger! Roger, I am sorry that I did not come back to care for you. It is my fault you are gone. I should have saved you!" he cried.

Hedyn's tears turned to uncontrolled sobs. He had not wept so since he was a babe. The guilt he felt for not being at Roger's side when he was needed most stabbed deeply at his heart. He was far from home in a hostile land. He felt utterly alone. Through his sobs he heard an ox cart jingle to a stop. "Business is lively—very lively, I must say," Snaggletooth Man said in the distance.

# CHAPTER THIRTEEN

**The Siege lines of Harfleur**
**Normandy, France**
**15 September 1415**

The Altarnon men grumbled as they sat in camp putting together rigid bundles of sticks called fascines. The bundles were heavy, three feet long, and a foot and a half in diameter. "We eat, we dig, we dodge quarrels, we sleep, and then we get up and do it all over again. Rumors fly as fast as arrows, but even they grow tiresome," said an archer.

Denzel Crocker added to the complaint as he tossed a fascine into a growing pile. "King Henry said this siege would last a week, but we have been digging in the dirt like gophers for a month. Now he has us making fascines for God knows what purpose."

Hedyn looked at the men he had known all his life. When the siege had begun a month earlier, they had been relatively clean. Now they were filthy and unshaven. Their white surcoats were so discolored by the mud and dust that the red crosses on their chests and backs were barely visible. Faces were varnished brown by the summer sun and smoky campfires. He wondered if he appeared as wretched. Suddenly, his heart filled with sorrow as he remembered how bedraggled Roger had looked when the cart took him away. As much as he tried, he could not shake his loneliness.

Sir John's company grew smaller. A quarrel struck a man three days earlier. He had a painful wound in his shoulder but would survive. Two archers, a man-at-arms, and one of the women cooks died of the bloody flux and were buried somewhere in the burying ground. Thomas and the dead cook's husband lay sick beneath a brush arbor in camp.

Everyone fought dysentery. The soldiers made such frequent visits to the latrines that they discarded their trousers and leggings and went bare-bottomed. Only the long tails of their tunics covered their nakedness. This especially aided those on the front lines, who sometimes had to relieve themselves where they stood.

"How do you fare this day, lad?" Hedyn was shaken from his melancholy by William's question. All the men sensed and respected

Hedyn's sorrow, but only William Whitwell consoled him. The big archer took time each day to talk to him and try to ease his burden.

"I am tolerable. I do my duty and try not to think of it," the boy said.

"You are wise to do so. I have prayed to our Lord Jesus every day that he will send you peace. Send us all peace. We have lost many good friends."

"Do you not pray for victory also so we might leave this place?" Hedyn asked.

"Victory will be granted to King Henry if it is God's will. In the end, it is only each man's salvation that is important. Do you not think the French pray to the same God and to their own saints to bring victory? Which king is worthy of victory in God's eyes?"

Hedyn noticed that William never discussed his unusual views on God and the saints with anyone other than him. Were these ideas what made the abbot pursue him and what made him seem secretive around the other men?

Denzel got up, tossing a completed fascine into a pile. He sat down next to William. "What would you have us do now, William?" Denzel asked.

"You should have your dinner, but drink only ale or wine and eat only food that is cooked. That will keep you out of the burying ground. Then, tend our horses. See that they are fed and watered."

He turned to Hedyn. "You should help with the horses also. Someone needs to look after Roger's palfrey." William nodded his head up the lane. "Sir John and the squire come yonder. Maybe they bring news."

The men stood respectfully and gathered around Sir John. He removed his helmet and gave the men permission to sit. Squire John sat heavily on the ground, his armor clattering on the way down. He took his helmet off wearily and revealed sunken eyes and a pale face. Hedyn could detect the same look of illness that he had seen in Roger's eyes. His heart raced. Was Squire John ill now also?

"I bring news," Sir John began. "King Henry is arranging shipping for our sick. They will be sent home where they may have a chance at survival. They are only a burden to the army here."

The men leaned forward to hear. "Our three sick archers, including Thomas Kelnystok, will be going home. Also, our last cook is sick and her husband is dead of the flux. She will go too." Sir John faced William. "William Whitwell of Devon, you will be the new ventenar." He addressed the archers again. "You men have already been turning to William for guidance since Thomas has been ill. He has proven to be a reliable man, and he has experience fighting the French."

The archers nodded their agreement.

Jan Tregeagle stood suddenly. "Whitwell is not an Altarnon man. The new ventenar must be an Altarnon man!"

Everyone turned and looked at Tregeagle in surprise.

"Shut up, Jan" The words came from Squire John in a flurry. "You hate Whitwell because he embarrassed you with a wooden poleaxe back in Altarnon. You have no say, so sit down." Tregeagle stiffened in indignation. The men stifled smiles as he sat without a word.

"I see you have finished the fascines." Sir John nodded to the pile of bundles.

"Aye, my Lord. I have also told the men to tend to their horses after they find victuals," William explained.

"Excellent. I have business to attend; I must find some other company who can share their cook." Sir John turned and strolled away.

As the men dispersed, Hedyn walked to where Squire John still rested on the ground. "May I speak with you, Squire John?"

The squire looked up at him and said, "Yes, I suppose."

Hedyn sat by his side. "Squire, are you well?

"Of course I am well!" The squire said indignantly.

Hedyn did not know how to express his concern without angering the squire. "It is just that. . . I am just concerned that you . . . remain well. It may be wise if you return with the sick to England." As the last word left his lips, Hedyn knew that his suggestion had come out too strong.

The squire jumped to his feet and then wobbled slightly until he found his balance. "I do not have the flux." He shook his finger in Hedyn's face. "I am quite well, and if you say anything to my father about this you will regret it!" He turned, stumbled, and stalked away.

Hedyn rolled to his knees and crossed himself. He began a prayer to Saint Nonna, but then he paused. He began again, "Please, Christ Jesus, protect my friend from the bloody flux. I swear I will do all in my power to keep him well. I will not let him down as I did Roger." He made the sign of the cross again and then hurried to catch up with his company.

*   *   *

He just wished they would shut up. If they would just be quiet, he could sleep. The complaint raced through his sleepy mind as Hedyn tried to get the rest he needed so badly. A kick to his feet woke him with a start. "Wake up, boy! The French have come out of their walls and are attacking!" Hedyn could not see through the dark, but he knew the voice. It was William.

"Go to the baggage train and fetch as many sheaves of arrows as you can carry. Bring them back here and wait until I send for you. I know not where this fight will take us, so do not try to follow."

"Yes, I will go now." Hedyn came to his feet quickly and rubbed the haze of sleep from his eyes. William was already gone. Shouts, some in French, surrounded him from all sides. A fire near the front line began to burn fiercely. A swirl of sparks raced to the heavens. The fire cast a dome of yellow light where dark forms of men seemed to scurry in every direction.

Crowded with servants, women, boys, and wagoners, the baggage train revealed utter chaos. Some of the men stood with swords drawn in case the French made it through the English lines. A crowd of boys tore the canvas from several carts to get at the arrows since there was no one left in charge to issue them. Each boy was on the same mission, to find arrows for his archers.

Hedyn carried away six sheaves, all that he could manage without a sack to carry them in. He stumbled back to camp with his arms full and stacked the sheaves neatly. He sat on the pile of fascines and waited. Father Stephen joined him.

"Is it safe here? Should we not go farther to the rear in case the French should break through?" Father Stephen craned his neck and strained to look through the darkness as he spoke.

"My ventenar told me to fetch arrows and to wait here. That is what I shall do," Hedyn replied calmly.

Father Stephen said, "Very well, then I am certain we are safe. I shall wait here with you." His trembling voice belied his lack of conviction.

A great tumult of shouts, screams, and the sound of metal on metal roared across the land. Hedyn wanted desperately to find his archers and to see what was happening. Instead, he followed his orders.

After an hour, the noise of battle diminished. Most of the fires were extinguished or had burned themselves out. A wounded man appeared from the darkness nearby. Father Stephen gasped then looked sheepishly at Hedyn after he realized the man posed no threat. Other men began to drift past them as they made their way to the rear.

"Did you see Sir John Trelawny's company?" Hedyn called out to one man who cradled a bleeding arm with his good one.

"If'n I did, I wouldn't have known it," he called back. "It was too dark to see me own company! I couldn't tell who I was swingin' me sword at most of the time."

Hedyn squirmed with impatience. The sound of battle had ceased, and only an occasional shout drifted through the night. Excited voices came to his ears before he saw Sir John's company appear from the dark into the dim starlight of the camp. He was especially relieved when he recognized the forms of Squire John and William Whitwell.

"We gave them a thrashing, we did!" Sir John said. "They'll not leave the safety of their walls again, I'll wager." Sir John looked around. "Do we have everyone?" The men looked around.

"I don't see Jan Tregeagle," Denzel offered.

78

"Aye," Sir John said. "When was the last time any of you saw Tregeagle?"

"Last I seen him was just before we got at the Frenchies that was around the big gonne," another man answered. At that moment, Jan Tregeagle strolled into camp from the opposite direction from where the others had approached.

The others looked at him as he came to a stop among them. "I got separated from the company. I've been fighting over on the left," he said before anyone asked him. Sir John nodded to him doubtfully but did not respond to his story. Hedyn wondered why Tregeagle came from the right of the line if he had been fighting on the left.

"You heard the orders that were given to us earlier. We will move out two hours before daylight. I guess we know now why we were ordered to make fascines. Make your peace with God, and try to get some rest," Sir John announced.

Several of the men formed a line in front of Father Stephen to receive absolution. Hedyn noticed that many of them pressed a coin into the priest's hand as they knelt before him.

Hedyn came to his feet as William approached him. "You did not need the arrows?" Hedyn asked.

"Too dark to shoot much. We did most of our fighting with sword and poleaxe this night. You would have been proud of how your Altarnon men fought."

Hedyn suspected that William had actually sent him to the baggage train to keep him out of danger. He felt disappointed and relieved at the same time.

The big archer put something heavy into Hedyn's hands. "These are the smallest that I could find," William said.

Hedyn held an old sheet iron helmet and a mail tunic up in the starlight to see them better. The breast of the mail bore a ragged hole and the heavy links were sticky. It took a moment for Hedyn to realize it was soaked in drying blood.

"A bascinet and hauberk?" he asked.

"Aye, you shall need these before this night is done."

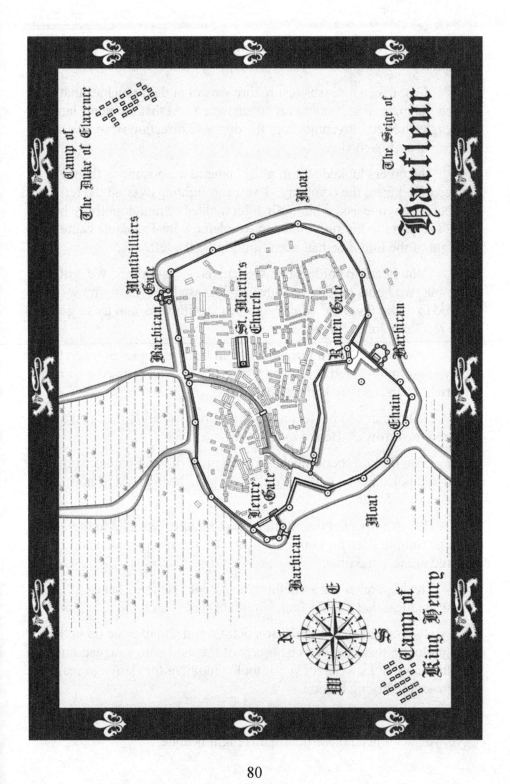

The Siege of Harfleur

Camp of
The Duke of Clarence

Montivilliers Gate

Barbican

St. Martin's Church

Moat

Rouen Gate

Barbican

Chain

Leure Gate

Moat

Barbican

Camp of
King Henry

# CHAPTER FOURTEEN

**Before the Leure Gate**
**Harfleur, France**
**16 September 1415**

Hedyn looked up. There, at the top of the fortification, was a yellow sphere of light floating along like a specter. In the black of the night, he had to remind himself it was nothing more than a Frenchman making his rounds. Grunting, he worked his way to a more comfortable position as he lay on his belly in the shallow trench. While he could see no farther than the archers beside him, he nonetheless felt the presence of hundreds of men and boys, fascines at the ready, awaiting the signal to advance. The Leure Gate and the surrounding moat sat invisible, two hundred and fifty paces in front of them.

Whispers punctuated the night air. William crawled through the trench on his hands and knees, stopping every few feet to repeat his orders.

"There will be a signal and we shall all rise and go at the same time. It will be too dark for the French to see you, but they will shoot just the same. You will not stop and use your bow. Instead, run forward and throw your fascines as far as you can into the water. Bridge the moat with fascines so our knights can cross at daybreak. Do this thing quickly, lads. If you do it well, we will not have to do it again when morning breaks."

"Shall Sir John be going with us?" one man asked.

"No, he and his men-at-arms will stay here until it is time to attack. We must fill that moat quickly," William answered.

"They need to keep those crossbomen's heads down. Will any of our archers be shooting at the walls when we go?" Denzel asked.

"Aye, from the trench behind us." William answered. "But run low. You don't want one of King Henry's arrows sticking in your arse." The men chuckled nervously at William's warning. William gave Hedyn's foot an encouraging squeeze as he crawled by.

But Hedyn needed more than encouragement. His mind raced with details. He tried to calculate how long it would take him to run to the moat, throw his fascine, and run back while under a shower of quarrels. Half a minute, a minute, two minutes if he stumbled in the dark? His heart turned heavy. Fear began to rise in his throat like bile. He checked his helmet again. While too big for him, he was grateful to have it. He only wished his entire body could be encased in steel.

Were his boots tied? Was his belt tight around his new hauberk? Was his fascine properly bundled? He had to pee, and his bladder ached. He suddenly realized that he was just as afraid of pissing himself in front of the men as he was of being killed by a French crossbow.

Feeble starlight illuminated the no-man's land. Every rock and stump cast low shadows like deep inky pools of blackness on the ground. The grinding of time had no mercy. *Will we ever do this thing*, he thought. Without a moon, he could not judge the passage of time. He wanted to scream his impatience.

A far-away voice called out, "Up, lads! Up! For England and Saint George!" Voices all along the trenches echoed the command.

Sir John shouted, "Men of Cornwall! Up! Up!" The archers scrambled to their feet. Like soldiers everywhere battling both enemies and fear, they shouted. They shouted until their voices echoed from the walls of Harfleur.

"Saint Geooooorge! For England and Saint Geooorge!"

Hedyn tried to add his voice to the appeal to the patron saint of England as well, but only a pathetic squeak escaped his parched throat. Four bounding steps from the trench, he tripped over his own fascine and slammed to his belly on the hard ground. By the time he regained his footing, the other archers were far ahead of him.

" L'Anglais, l'Anglais! Shouts from the wall told him that the French were fighting back. Enemy crossbowmen tossed torches, some of which cleared the water and landed on dry ground. Small circles of yellow light penetrated the darkness where they fell. The men and boys carrying their stick bundles crowded away from the threat of certain death.

Hedyn sprinted, carrying the fascine against his chest for protection. A quarrel buzzed past his ear and he swatted at it as though it were a bee. More buzzing told him the air was filled with deadly missiles.

As he passed a man holding the feathered end of a quarrel that protruded from his chest, another quarrel struck home. It sounded like a meat ax falling into joint of mutton.

Soon, he passed men scurrying back after throwing their fascines and completing their mission. They made no more self-encouraging shouts to Saint George. They had survived, and now they celebrated by laughing and hooting like boys during an All Hallows Eve prank.

Hedyn ran on in the dark, almost alone, until he stumbled on fascines in the middle of the moat. He hurriedly heaved his bundle of sticks as far as he could and turned to run. Throwing away his load lent a new nimbleness to his feet. He splashed through the shallow water that covered the bridge of sticks. Frenchmen shot blindly at his noisy retreat. Quarrels buzzed and hissed around him. When he reached dry land, he breathed a sigh of relief. He thought he was safe. Just then, a torch thumped at the front of his scrambling feet and enveloped him in a circle of sickly yellow light. Immediately, a great blow struck him on the back of his head, as hard as a club on the skull of a slaughtered lamb.

All light, all sound, and all awareness left Hedyn as the impact threw him to the ground.

# CHAPTER FIFTEEN

**Before the Leure Gate**
**Harfleur, France**
**16 September 1415**

Hedyn was not quite awake, but he knew that his throat was parched and his head pounded. He sensed something approaching, something big and noisy. As the noise grew, he began to stir. Finally, opening one eye, he gasped at the brilliance of the dawn sun that was just clearing the town walls. New pain shot through his temples, and then he smelled the acrid odor of stale urine. He had pissed himself after all. After his eyes focused, he saw a crossbow quarrel sticking in the ground a few inches from his face. He remembered where he was.

The noise grew louder, and Hedyn recognized the sound of voices and the clank of armor. Just as William had told him, the English assault started at first light. He stretched his neck to see a line of a thousand men-at-arms approaching the Leure Gate. The organized line began to collapse as the men crowded in to make the attack. The shouts of "Saint Geooorge!" and "King Henry!" failed to drown out the sound of French quarrels as they buzzed over his head like a swarm of angry hornets.

Hedyn lay near the moat in full view of the men on the walls. He closed his eyes and remained perfectly still, hoping that the attacking men-at-arms would draw all attention away from him.

A thunder of footsteps came upon him. Someone stepped on the edge of his arm, and he reflexively jerked it away. The owner of the foot laughed and said, "A live one!" Another man, close upon the heels of the first, shouted, "Get up, boy, and run! Quit this place as fast as you can!"

Hedyn needed no further encouragement. When he got to his feet he wobbled but soon found his balance. His head hurt and he squinted to block the painful light, but he headed toward the English lines as swiftly as he could. His only thought was to escape the battle and the French crossbows.

Hedyn came to a trench and stumbled in among archers, thinking they were his own company. When he heard the heavy Yorkshire accents, he realized otherwise. They laughed heartily as he tried to get away. One of the men said, "You cannot outrun that quarrel, lad!" Another pointed to the back of his helmet. "Aye, I reckon that one has already caught you!"

Hedyn reached behind his helmet, finding the shaft and fletching of a quarrel embedded in the sheet steel. He slid the helmet off and stared in disbelief at the missile. One of the York men took the helm and held it aloft for the others to see.

"Your old helm has saved your life this day, I wager." He wiggled the iron point from the helmet and tossed the quarrel out of the trench. "Were you one of the men who filled the moat with fascines this morning?"

*One of the men?* Hedyn thought. No one had ever grouped him among men before. He only squinted and nodded dumbly.

"I reckon I'd have messed me britches if I was made to do the likes of that!" the man spouted.

One of his mates called out, "You messed your britches anyway, Ventenar!"

The man looked sheepish and whispered to Hedyn, "I've a bit of the camp disease, you see." The archers roared with laughter.

The York man pulled Hedyn to his feet and pointed at the Leure Gate. "See what you have accomplished with your bridge of sticks?" Hedyn watched as hundreds of men-at-arms swarmed across the moat and up on the barbican. "I wager they will take that barbican this day. If so, we archers will be called to man the walls and pour arrows into the town. Then Henry can move his big gonnes right up to the Leure Gate and pound it to bits. The Frog Eaters will have no choice but to surrender to Henry and open the town to us. And it's your fascines what dunnit," the York man explained.

Hedyn tried to smile, but his throbbing head would not allow it. The French quarrel had only pricked his scalp when it stuck in the steel helmet, but the impact had jarred his brain.

"Do you know where the archers from Sir John Trelawny's company are now?" Hedyn squeaked out.

"French quarrels buzzed over his head like a swarm of angry hornets."

The York man thought for a moment, then said, "That company I do not know, lad. But those men who helped fill the moat this morning were allowed to return to camp for rest."

As he climbed from the trench, Hedyn mumbled a thank you over his shoulder. He stumbled on with his helmet under his arm and his eyes half closed. Longing to quench his thirst and rest his body, he thought about what the York man had told him and wondered if his part in the battle really would help bring victory. He did not notice the narrow trench. He half fell, half slid to its bottom with a thud. He was not alone. A man in full armor sat against the dirt wall, his head hidden from view. With a closed visor, he looked down at Hedyn. There was something familiar about the man-at-arms.

"Jan? Jan Tregeagle?" Hedyn sputtered. The man grabbed him by the hair and dragged him through the dirt to his side. Pain shot through Hedyn's head like an arrow. He screeched with new hurt. The steel scales on the armored gauntlet felt cold and sharp as the man pressed a hand over his mouth.

"Shut your pie hole, boy! Did Whitwell send you?" Tregeagle demanded.

Hedyn wiggled from under the heavy palm and pleaded, "No! No one sent me. I was only making my way back to camp!"

Tregeagle flipped up his visor and leaned over the boy. Sour spittle sprayed over Hedyn's face as Tregeagle snarled, "If you tell anyone you saw me here, I will cut you open from your crotch to your gullet!"

Hedyn's fear turned to outrage when he realized that Tregeagle had hidden to keep from fighting in the attack against the barbican.

Tregeagle tried a new tactic when Hedyn's face failed to register terror. "I have me a better idea. After I kill you, Tressa will be next. When I get back to Cornwall, your little sister will disappear one morning when she goes for water. By the time anyone finds her, she will be just a little pile of bones in the forest."

Tregeagle smiled triumphantly when he noted the fear in Hedyn's eyes. "Might have a bit of fun with her too before I do her in," he added. "You understand me, villein's son?" Hedyn nodded. Tregeagle poked

86

his head up above the trench wall and stole a glance. The battle still raged noisily on the barbican.

"I suppose I'll just wait here a bit longer. You be off, now. I'll be watching you. Remember, just a little pile of bones in the forest."

Hedyn climbed from the trench, still trembling from the encounter. He forgot his headache and the battle that raged behind him. He could only think of his sister and how heartbroken his parents would be if anything happened to Tressa. He could imagine Jago and Guenbrith frantically calling Tressa's name as they searched the Altarnon fields and woods for her. Before he knew it, he stumbled into his camp. Shouts and a sudden rush shook him from his thoughts.

"The boy! He is alive!" A voice called out.

"By the bones of the saints, Hedyn lives!" Father Stephen cried as he ran to Hedyn's side. All of the Altarnon archers crowded around him.

All the men laughed and talked excitedly. They nudged him and slapped his back in joy.

William tussled his matted hair. "Someone saw you fall, lad. We thought we had lost you. What's this?" He took Hedyn's punctured helmet from his hands and stuck his finger in the hole where the quarrel had struck.

Father Stephen saw the hole and exclaimed, "Saint Nonna was surely with you this morning!" William just smiled and said, "Christ himself was by your side."

Denzel added, "Peew! You stink to the heavens, lad. I fear you have fallen into a cesspit! We will take you to the river and let you wash the stink from yourself. Did you see that moat, boy? I knew those fascines would do the job!"

The men laughed, and Hedyn forced a smile. He wanted desperately to tell them of Tregeagle hiding in the trench. But the words "just a little pile of bones in the forest" silenced him.

# CHAPTER SIXTEEN

**In Sir John's Camp**
**Harfleur, France**
**17 September 1415**

When the sound of battle abated, a great cheer echoed from the town walls. What started as a few hoots and shouts built into a roar that filled the air between Harfleur and the English camps. The cheer could mean only one thing: the English had taken the Leure Gate.

The archers were called back to the front after their morning rest. William made Hedyn remain in camp by assigning him a list of chores. Hedyn bristled at first; after all, those were HIS archers, and he should be with them.

Father Stephen joined him when he stopped his work to look toward the cheering. "They have surely taken the gate! Will they be coming back to camp now, you wonder?" the priest asked.

"I know not. I hope all come back—back and alive," Hedyn answered.

Hedyn busied himself polishing Sir John's extra armor. He scoured the metal with an old rag and a handful of sand and tried not to think about the battle at the Leure Gate. *Were they all safe? Had any been wounded or killed? Would he see Squire John and William again?* No news came from the front. Hedyn thought he would burst with impatient anxiety.

As the shadows lengthened in the late afternoon, an ox cart trundled into camp followed by Sir John, William, and two of the archers. Hedyn dropped the helmet he polished and ran to meet them.

"Where are the others?" Hedyn cried out. Sir John and the archers ignored him and reached into the bed of the cart. When he heard a groan, Hedyn jumped up and stood on the spokes of the cart wheel so he could see inside. Squire John's eyes fluttered. The archers lifted him and slid him to the rear of the cart. His father sat him up and cradled him in his arms.

"I found him unconscious as the fighting waned around the gate. I first thought him dead, but I could find no wound or blood on his body.

He is ill. My poor boy is very ill," Sir John explained to Hedyn. The archers took him from his father and removed his plate armor piece by piece. They gently lifted him, carried him into his tent, and placed him on a cot. Hedyn stood aside dumbly. He could tell that none of the men knew what to do for him.

One of the archers saw Hedyn's crestfallen face and said, "By the Saints, none of our other friends have met with scathe. Jan Tregeagle became separated in the dark and fought with another company. He rejoined us this afternoon. Sir John has left him in charge of the rest of the company."

The mention of Tregeagle brought the terror of their dawn meeting back to Hedyn. He wanted to scream "Tregeagle was not separated! He cowered in a hole to avoid the battle! He is a coward!" But Tregeagle's threat came back to him—"just a little pile of bones in the forest." He remained silent and did not tell what he knew.

Hedyn heard Squire John cough and groan inside the canvas pavilion. Hedyn pushed Tregeagle out of his thoughts and turned his attention back to his sick friend. *I cannot lose another friend! There must be something I can do to help him!* He steeled his nerves and entered the tent uninvited.

Sir John knelt and stroked his son's face. After a long while he got to his feet, tears in his eyes, and went outside. He and Father Stephen stood a few paces away and prayed.

William pulled Hedyn to a far corner of the big tent and said softly, "Do you want to help your friend?" Hedyn nodded. "I will excuse you from all other duties if you will care for him."

"I will care for him even if I have other duties. I will not let him down like. . ." Hedyn's voice trailed off. He thought of Roger. He spent many days worrying about the sickness that only he could see growing in his friend. He had vowed to himself that he would save the squire should the flux strike. But now that sickness came, he wondered if he could keep his vow.

William put his hand on the boy's shoulder. "Know this," he said. "When a man dies of the flux, he dies of thirst. Not the thirst of the tongue that we think of, but his whole body dies for lack of water. Everything he drinks is spewed back or spills from his rear end. If this boy is to survive, you must keep giving him drink, and food too, even if his gut will not hold it." The archer bent low to look in Hedyn's eyes. "If he cannot keep drink inside, he will surely perish. Do you understand?"

Hedyn nodded. "Aye. I understand. I will do it," he said. He trembled with the responsibility.

"Sir John wanted to send the boy back to England on the next ship, but I have persuaded him otherwise. The boy will not get the care with strangers that he will receive here. He would die before they reach land again."

Squire John moaned, and his cot squeaked as he moved restlessly. William looked at him with worried eyes.

"The French have sent their heralds to King Henry to seek terms for surrender. The siege will be over soon. Until then, neither Sir John nor I will have any time to assist you. Stay with him. Keep something in his belly. If he begins to hold things in his belly and to pee again, then he may survive."

"Pee again? I don't understand."

"The sickness is preventing his innards from working properly. If he pees, that means his body is using the water as it should. I must go. I will keep both of you in my prayers."

*   *   *

The September sun bore down on the canvas roof, radiating heat. Hedyn sat dozing with his head in his hands. When Squire John stirred, Hedyn's eyes popped open. He turned toward his friend, noting the sweat that poured from John's face. With Hedyn looking on, John shivered as though the coldest day of winter raged outside. He grunted and jerked his knees to his chest as another massive cramp squeezed his guts like a giant fist. Growling through gritted teeth, he struggled with the pain. Finally, the monster in his belly relaxed its grip.

Renewed stink exploded in the tent as the squire soiled himself again. Red diarrhea stains on the boy's legs confirmed that John's illness had turned to the bloody flux. He turned and retched into the rushes that covered the tent floor. Squire John coughed as he vomited the sour wine. Hedyn tried not to recoil as spittle and wine sprayed his face.

"I cannot take this sour wine, Hedyn! It makes me retch," John said breathlessly. He held himself up on one elbow momentarily before falling back.

"Squire, would you try some ale again?" Hedyn asked desperately.

"Nay, the ale is sour too. I cannot abide the ale either." Both the wine and the ale supplies were indeed sour and stale. Wooden casks could not protect the freshness of the drinks after long days in the summer sun. Although they did not taste good, they would not cause sickness like the water in the nearby streams and rivers. But for the squire, who already had extreme nausea and diarrhea, the sour wine and ale only aggravated his condition.

"But, Squire, you must drink something. You must keep drink in your belly to get better."

"If only I had a cup of water from Saint Nonna's well. Remember how we would push our whole face into that well pond and drink when we were children playing on the green? I dreamed of us drinking there. But when we went back for more, the well was dry! Oh, for a drink of the Saint's water." The squire's voice trailed off as he lapsed back into a fretful sleep.

Hedyn gently removed the course linen bedclothes from the cot and wiped the squire's legs with a wet cloth. He would rinse the stinky and bloody sheet in the river and hang it to dry. Another sheet, already dry and fluttering on a tree branch, would replace it. He did this every morning and again in the afternoon. He had little time to clean himself. His cloths reeked of sickness. He wondered if he would carry the smell forever.

Hedyn pushed the canvas door away and stumbled from the tent. The breeze cleared the smell from his nose for a moment. The squire's cry for water occupied all of his thoughts. Tears left white trails through the brown dirt on his cheeks. How could he fetch water from Saint Nonna's well? How could he find any water that did not come from the stinking streams around the camp?

91

He walked slowly to the woman who had been hired to cook for Sir John's company. Hedyn hated talking to her. She had a sour disposition and complained about any request made of her. Her tangled hair escaped in clumps from under a linen cap and the seams of her clothing stretched to bursting. While everyone else in camp grew thin from hard work and poor food, she alone grew fat.

"You stink like the latrine, boy," she said as she wrinkled her nose. "What do you want?"

"I need porridge for Squire John," Hedyn managed to squeak out.

The large woman poured water from a wooden bucket into a cauldron over an open fire. "I've just brought this here water from the river. It has to boil, and then I'll throw in the barley to cook. It will be an hour yet before its ready," she announced. "'Sides, it will do him no good. He'll just throw it up or squirt it down his leg. They tell me the squire will die. You're wastin' good porridge."

Hedyn just looked at her dumbly, and thought that she must be the cruelest woman in all of England.

"Come find me when it boils, then I'll put in the barley." She turned and waddled to a canvas awning where she lay down on a pallet of blankets. Within a few minutes, she snored like the burliest of archers.

Hedyn looked into the cauldron. A few tendrils of vapor swirled from the water as it heated. Hedyn watched the heating water and remembered his conversation with Roger during the hot march from Altarnon to Plymouth. *Why wouldn't ale, porridge, pottage and other cooked things cause illness when ordinary water would? What did they all have in common? They all boiled water as part of their cooking!* Ale and freshly cooked things would not make a man sick, no matter where the water came from. He remembered what the brewer had told him at the River Tamar. He said that Saint Brigid, the patron saint of ale, changed the water and made it safe to drink. Hedyn had no faith in Saint Brigid but decided that he would cook the water and see if the sickness left it. He would take the squire cooked water and hope that the sick boy would keep it down.

Hedyn tiptoed around the camp kitchen looking for a small pot. He knocked over a bundle of firewood and froze, but the old cook just snorted and continued to snore. At last, he found a small copper kettle. He dared not ask to borrow the kettle for fear the cook would declare him an idiot and deny him its use. He took the pot back to the fire and waited and waited some more. The water would never get hot, he thought. He glanced back and forth from the cauldron to the sleeping cook, hoping that the water would boil before she stirred. He added wood to the fire so the flames licked up the sides of the big pot.

At last bubbles appeared, and soon after, the water rolled and splashed as it came to full boil. Hedyn tried to scoop some water with the kettle, but the heat from the fire and the spouting hot water drove him back. He finally tossed the kettle into the pot and fished it out by the bail with a long stick.

"The water boils," Hedyn called out as he started back to Squire John's tent. He ran far out of sight before the cook rolled off of her pile of blankets.

*   *   *

While the water cooled, Hedyn sat by John's side for an hour, watching him sleep. Finally it cooled enough to drink. He scooped a bit out with an earthen cup and drank it. *Tastes like ordinary water,* he thought. He gently squeezed John's sweaty shoulder.

"Squire, would you take some water?" Hedyn asked.

Squire John licked his parched lips. "Yes, water would do well," he croaked. Hedyn helped him sit up and held the cup to his lips. John took all the water with one gulp. Hedyn's eyes grew in astonishment. He dipped the cup again and John took all of it, slower this time than the first. John coughed and Hedyn thought for sure that John would vomit the water up, like he had done the wine and ale. To his surprise, the water stayed in the boy's belly. John soon settled and went back to sleep.

Each time John awoke, Hedyn encouraged him to drink. He built a small fire near the tent and cooked his own water. He only returned to the camp kitchen to fetch food.

"Some rascal has made away with my little kettle! Have you seen my copper kettle, about the size of a knight's helmet?" The cook asked every visitor to her fire. Hedyn just shook his head and held out a

93

wooden trencher on which the cook plopped down a mound of sticky barley porridge.

As the next days passed, fewer cramps plagued Squire John. He began to eat more and eagerly drained the clay cup when Hedyn offered it to him. His vomiting and diarrhea eased. More and more of the water and food stayed in John's belly. Hedyn could see John's progress. Cooking the water worked, but he had no idea why. *Could Saint Brigid be changing the water after all?*

Hedyn sat by his little fire, near his camp but far away from the fat cook. He watched the little copper kettle as it finally came to a slow boil. Something rustled behind him. "Should have known it was you who stole that kettle. Villeins can't be trusted." Jan Tregeagle stood behind him with his hands on his hips. "I'll have that kettle," he said, as he kicked it from the fire. The embers sizzled where the water splashed. Hedyn jumped to his feet. "That water was for Squire John," he retorted indignantly.

Tregeagle stepped over the fire and pushed Hedyn to the ground. "Ha! Are you to shave him? What use does that boy have of boiling water? He will be dead in a few days. The cook has been looking for this kettle. I'll take it back to her and get a nice joint of meat as a reward." Tregeagle picked up the hot kettle with his gloved hand. He strolled away without looking back at Hedyn.

Hedyn trembled with rage. He knew that as a villein he held no power over the man-at-arms. Tregeagle was a coward and a bully. He may also be capable of murder, as he had suggested during their confrontation during the battle of the Leure Gate. Hedyn sat by the fire and stared at the steaming ashes. *What am I to do with no kettle? How am I to make Squire John well without it?*

The cook had described the copper kettle as "the size of a knight's helmet," he remembered. A thought came to him. He jumped to his feet and sprinted to the brush arbor where he stored his meager belongings. He picked up his helmet and examined it, and then saw the hole left by the French quarrel. It would hold no water. He went to the baggage cart and rummaged through the extra armor taken from the dead Altarnon men. An ancient old helm with a flat top caught his attention. He smiled. It was perfect. Within an hour, boiling water bubbled in the inverted helmet up to the eye slits.

94

"An ancient old helm with a flat top caught his attention. He smiled. It was perfect. Within an hour, boiling water bubbled in the inverted helmet up to the eye slits."

95

The third day after Hedyn first cooked the water, the squire slept through the entire night without cramping or throwing up.

"Hedyn, wake up!" Squire John leaned from his cot and roughly shook Hedyn to wake him from a deep sleep.

"Wha...what is the matter?" Hedyn answered groggily.

"I need to make water! Help me up so I can go out to pee," the squire commanded with renewed authority.

Hedyn jumped to his feet in his excitement. "You have to pee! You have to pee! The squire must pee!"

Squire John looked at Hedyn as though he had gone mad. "Just help me up so I can go to the privy."

Hedyn pulled the Squire to his feet and looped his arm around his neck. He half dragged the boy to the tent door. A bedraggled troop of archers streamed by the tent on their way to some place of rest. "Make way! Make way! The squire has to pee!" The men parted as the two boys pushed through the crowd. Hedyn did not hear the laughter and catcalls of the passing archers. He felt a joy in his heart that had been absent for a very long time.

# PART THREE
## The Battle of Agincourt

*Agincourt, Agincourt!*
*Know ye not Agincourt?*
*Never to be forgot*
*Or known to no men?*
*Where English cloth-yard arrows*
*Kill'd the French like tame sparrows,*
*Slaine by our bowmen.*

Bowman's Glory. c. 1600

# CHAPTER SEVENTEEN

**Harfleur, France**
**1 October 1415**

Squire John sat in the shade of a large oak tree and studied the Altarnon men as they fed their horses. There was new color in John's cheeks, replacing the deathly pallor that had once tinged his beardless face. Harfleur, what little of it that remained intact, had become an English town.

King Henry received the surrender of Harfleur with great pomp and ceremony on September 23. The military and civic leaders of town paraded to his throne, set up on the highest ground of the English camp. Ropes trailed behind each of them with nooses tight around their necks. Their very lives were in Henry's hands. But Henry showed mercy. No lives were forfeited. The gates of the city were thrown open, but the king did not allow his army to rampage through the streets killing and plundering. Instead, Henry expelled only those inhabitants who would not accept him as their king and sovereign.

In the days after the surrender, a pitiful line of refugees streamed from the town, taking only what they could carry on their backs.

Now there was rest, and the weary English army regained its strength on renewed supplies of food, ale, and wine. Sir John had claimed the abandoned home of a merchant, and for the first time in six weeks, his men enjoyed a roof over their heads and straw pallets under their backs every night.

After a dawn breakfast, the archers marched to the horse corrals outside the town walls. They spent the time feeding and grooming their neglected mounts. The palfreys were each tied along a picket line stretched several yards between the trees on the edge of a field. The men brushed coats and cleaned out hooves as the horses munched on hay. Hedyn's old mare had finally become his friend. Instead of bared teeth, she now greeted him with a whinny and lowered her head so he could scratch between her ears.

Hedyn sat by Squire John's side. He smiled as one of the archers made another wild boast about his skills as a bowman. Soon, all of the men drifted away from the picket line and started practicing with their bows.

Squire John grumbled, "I should be with my father. He is at King Henry's tent this very moment. All the knights are there making plans. He took Jan Tregeagle with him and sent me here to supervise the archers. I don't know what my father sees in Tregeagle. He should be here instead of me."

Hedyn stiffened with the mention of Tregeagle's name. *Should I say what I know about Tregeagle?* he thought. But Tregeagle's threat, "just a little pile of bones in the forest," resonated through his mind. Instead, he changed the subject so he would not hear the name again.

"Could I get you anything else, Squire? A cup of ale or a crust of bread mayhap?" Hedyn asked.

"Nay. I think I've have eaten more today than any day since I fell ill. I'll just enjoy this shade a bit longer," the squire replied. "What about you, Hedyn? Your bow is on your back, but you do not shoot at marks like the rest of the men."

Hedyn looked at the group of archers as they took turns shooting at a stake in the ground a hundred paces distant. A round of cheers went up as William Whitwell's arrow glanced off the stake before burying itself into the hard, dry summer soil.

"I will stay by your side should you require anything, Squire," Hedyn answered. *I can hardly pull my bow, much less hit a distant mark,* he thought. He had not even taken his new bow from its case in over a week.

Hedyn noticed a shadow fall over him. When he looked up, the presence of three men startled him. The man in front was short but powerfully built with long hair tied behind his head and a thick, curly, black beard. He leaned on what looked to Hedyn like a long board with a small bow fastened crosswise near its end. A crossbow! *So this is what a crossbow looks like up close.*

"I see by your clothing that you are a man of rank. Do you command this band of archers, Lord?" he asked Squire John in heavily accented English. Hedyn thought there was something familiar about his accent.

"I do command these men. You are not English. Who, pray tell, are you?" the squire asked, trying not to sound surprised at the arrival of strangers.

"I am Charles of Brest. I come from Brittany to join King Henry, my sovereign, in fighting the French," he explained.

Hedyn realized why the man's accent sounded familiar.

"You sound like a Cornishman!" Hedyn exclaimed.

Charles laughed. "I suppose that I do. My native tongue is Breton. It is very much like Cornish, but not enough for you to understand, methinks."

After noticing the strangers, William and the other archers gathered around.

"What brings you to us, Charles of Brest?" the squire asked.

"Ah, yes. For many years I have heard boasts of the English, with their crooked sticks and tales of how far and straight they can shoot. My comrades and I spied your men here shooting. I would like to shoot my arbalest against your best bowman," Charles answered.

Denzel Crocker piped up indignantly as he pulled his fingers through his whiskers, "Christ's bones, man! Crooked sticks? There are a lot of dead Frenchmen who lost their lives to these crooked sticks!"

"Mayhap," Charles replied. "But why should a man strain to bend such a stick when I can shoot straighter, farther, and with greater power with my crossbow without such work? My goat's foot will do the work for me." He patted a long metal rod with a hinged, forked end that hung from his belt.

"Why, that is no more than a board with a child's bow nailed to it. I wager a woman could point and shoot that bow as easy as a man. I have some silver to place against your purse!" Denzel exclaimed. The other men added to the din of voices and began gathering their silver to match the Breton's purse.

Squire John leaned back against the oak. "Ventenar, if it pleases, you can pick an archer and contest this man. I'll only observe," John said.

Hedyn noticed a wry smile flash across William's face and then disappear. "I know not who we should choose to shoot against you. We are all good archers, but no champions," he offered.

"Mayhap it should be yourself," the Breton suggested. "After all, you are the ventenar and the biggest of these men. We will see how you fare."

The men murmured consent. "But, pray tell, what is the nature of your wager? What shall we shoot?" William asked.

"That stump yonder across the field will serve well as a mark to shoot," Charles said. The recently cut wood shone bone-white in the afternoon light.

William shielded his eyes against the sun and squinted. "I think I discern something yon," and pointed several yards to the right of the target. Hedyn could see the stump clearly and was sure that William's keen eyes could see it also. Then he thought, *Why is William pretending not to see the mark?*

"No, No. There! That stump," Charles said impatiently and pointed over William's shoulder.

William stood up straight and turned to Charles and said, "Ah, that stump. That is a long shoot! A much longer shoot than I expected," William exclaimed.

"It is a fair shoot, a fair shoot!" one of the Breton's friends offered.

William put his hand to his chin, as though he was considering something. "Would you deign to double our wager if I. . ." William stopped in mid-sentence. "No, I should not risk these men's coins on such a notion."

"By all means, Ventenar, finish your challenge. Pray tell how you might double the wager," the Breton urged.

"I was going to suggest that I not use my own bow, that I would pick another bow from the least of us to shoot, if you would double the wager." William looked around at each of his archers as if searching for a likely substitute for his bow. Finally he pointed beyond them to Hedyn, who still lounged by the squire's side.

101

"You, boy!"   Hedyn looked up with wide eyes, and then looked behind him to make sure that he was the boy that William addressed. He slowly pointed to himself.

"Yes, you. Bring me the bow that is upon your back," the ventenar demanded.

Hedyn jumped to his feet and took the bow case from his back and quickly slid his bow free of the canvas. He trotted to William and placed the bow in his hands.

William looked at the bow in his hands. "Oh," William said, as if surprised and disappointed.

"Nay! You shan't search for another! That is the bow you have chosen to double the wager," Charles said impatiently.

William sighed. "Aye, so it is," William said as he strung the bow. "But I request one other condition on this wager. The winner shall not be he who first strikes the stump. The winner shall be the first man who strikes it two times."

Charles looked at William suspiciously and then said, "So it will be." He leaned near his friends and said something in Breton. To Hedyn, he seemed to be reassuring his comrades.

All heads turned when Squire John called out, "How long is the shoot? How far away is your mark?"

"A fair question, Squire," Denzel answered. "Shall I pace it, Squire?" Squire John nodded, and the men watched patiently as Denzel began walking briskly in even steps across the field. At last he came to the stump. He cupped his hands around his mouth and called out, "Seven and thirty and one hundred paces." He trotted off to the side, safe out of the line of flight.

"Christ's bones, that is a long shoot for such a small target," one of the men exclaimed.

Charles scratched his head nervously, but William seemed unconcerned. One of the strangers asked Charles something in Breton with an anxious tone. Charles hushed him with a raised hand.

William and Charles stepped forward from the crowd with a few paces between them, as the archers and Bretons formed up so all could see across the field. William pulled five bodkin arrows from his arrow bag. He looked down the length of each to check for straightness. A wiggle of each goose feather ensured it was well attached. He stuck four of the arrows, point down, into the ground near his feet.

Hedyn watched in fascination as Charles removed the goat's foot lever that hung from his belt. He held the nose of the weapon down by placing his foot in a metal stirrup then used the lever to cock the heavy bowstring. Although the bow was very short compared to an English bow, Hedyn could tell that it held more power than the strongest yew. By the time the Breton was finished cocking and loading his crossbow, William had been waiting with a nocked arrow for half a minute.

Charles of Brest and William Whitwell of Devonshire looked at each other and nodded to indicate that all was in readiness to shoot. Charles tucked the butt of the crossbow under his right arm and sighted down the quarrel. He tripped a long lever under the stock, and the bow released with a sharp metallic twang. The quarrel disappeared so fast it seemed to vanish from the weapon.

William almost squatted to heave the long bow to its full draw, bending it farther than Hedyn imagined it could bend. He opened his string hand as it reached his right ear and the bow hummed like the string on an untuned musical instrument. The arrow arched high into the air as the men watched its flight.

The crossbow quarrel stuck into the ground a few feet to the left of the stump. Two seconds later, William's arrow embedded itself in the ground fifteen feet short and a few feet to the right. The Bretons cheered and the archers gasped. Charles smiled as he took his goat's foot from his belt to reload, certain of victory.

"Charles, I would like to add a gallon of Gascon wine to our wager," William announced suddenly. The crossbowman stopped and looked at William in disbelief and then looked at his friends. His comrades eagerly nodded approval. "Aye, a gallon of Gascon wine is added to the wager, as you say!" Charles said and grinned as he placed a quarrel on his crossbow.

Both men released their missiles simultaneously. The Breton waited to see his quarrel imbed itself squarely in the middle of the stump. But to his surprise, William had already loaded and shot all four of the arrows at his feet. The speed of his knocking and releasing of the arrows astonished even the most seasoned of the Altarnon men. Two arrows were still in flight when William's first bodkin pierced the hard dry wood of the stump. The next two struck home near the first, and the fourth arrow glanced off the Breton's quarrel and disappeared into the trees. William had nocked, aimed, and released four arrows in less than fifteen seconds.

The Altarnon men cheered and pounded William on the back. Even the squire joined in the merriment. The Bretons stood dumfounded as they tried to take in what had just happened. First anger then resignation passed over their faces.

Hedyn tugged at William's sleeve. "William, why my bow, and why did you take such a chance with it?" he asked. William bent and said so only Hedyn could hear, "Ha, I have handled your bow and know that Jago makes a fine staff—even if it does ride on a boy's back. But these men did not know that. After the first arrow fell short, I knew precisely how to aim the next. I knew the Breton could hit the mark, but I also knew that I could hit it faster the second time."

After the cheers died away, Charles approached Squire John and placed a leather purse filled with silver pennies in his hand. "Lord, I am the best crossbowman in Brest, and I feel that I have been blindly led to the slaughter by the best archer in England! Pride goeth before the fall."

"I hope you have no ill feelings, Charles of Brest. You are a fine shooter after all, but no crossbowman can shoot as fast as an English archer. The winnings will be divided among all my archers."

"No ill feelings, Lord. I will endeavor to bring a gallon of Gascon wine before the army marches."

All of the archers' attention was now drawn to the conversation. "Before the army marches? The army is to march?" William asked.

"Aye, have you not heard? It was decided this forenoon. King Henry will take his army overland to Calais. We march in a few days. Some say the French are gathering a large army to meet us. I pray that we can reach Calais before the French are upon us."

"William had nocked, aimed, and released four arrows in less than fifteen seconds."

# CHAPTER EIGHTEEN

**Arques, France**
**11 October 1415**

The Montivilliers Road connected Norman coastal towns from Harfleur, all the way north to the River Somme. It followed the coast across intermittent rolling hills, marshlands, and meager forests. From atop his old mare, Hedyn caught a glimmer of sunlight through the trees reflecting off the British Sea. The road neared the ocean once more. The column left the trees and rode into a broad plain of high grass.

A clear view of the sea opened up to Hedyn's west. He stretched forward in the saddle and scratched the palfrey between the ears as she plodded along. She turned her head to look at him with one eye, blew softly through her nose, and continued on. It pleased the boy that he and the old mare had made peace and become friends. It occurred to him that his horse had no name. *I will have to find the perfect name for her,* he thought.

Several cogs sailed north a few miles off the coast. Hedyn turned to William. "Ventenar, why did we not take shipping to Calais instead of going on land? Would it not have been faster and easier?"

"Aye," William answered. "Indeed, it would have been easier. But King Henry is making a point to the French that he can go anywhere he desires in what he considers his kingdom, and they can do nothing to stop him. To go back to England after taking Harfleur or to sail to Calais in safety might indicate fear on his part."

"More like vanity!" Denzel Crocker, spoke up from behind them. "Tis kingly vanity that takes us overland to Calais," he said in a low voice. "If he misjudges the French, they may cut us off and trounce us. Our army is much reduced; we have only nine hundred men-at-arms and five thousand archers left. The frogs can assemble five times that many men. Indeed, rumor has it that the dauphin even now assembles his army at Rouen."

Hedyn stood in his stirrups and pivoted in the saddle as they came to a low rise. Men and horses stretched as far as he could see in both directions along the Montivilliers Road. Henry divided the army into three divisions. The king commanded the center division, which included Sir John Trelawny's company. Sir John Cornewaille commanded the leading division and the Duke of York the rear guard.

One hundred and fifty miles separated Harfleur and Calais. Henry's lieutenants calculated that the army, marching twenty miles per day, would make the trip in eight days. To hurry things along, they had to leave behind the big gonnes and heavy baggage wagons. Speed was of the essence. Carts carried the king's and other nobleman's belongings, but the majority of the supplies and weapons were piled high on each extra horse. Of course, every man and every packhorse carried bundles of precious arrows.

"I have heard it said that our column includes twenty thousand horses." William broke the silence. Hedyn looked behind him again and then strained to see to his front. Every man sat on a horse and most led an extra mount piled high with arrows and provisions. He could also see small herds of coursers and palfreys urged along by boys and men.

"Only eight days of food were allowed. It is three days into this march, and half of it already is gone. If we don't get to Calais in eight days, I wager there will be some empty bellies among us," Denzel complained.

The conversation ended when loud voices sounded from their front. Hedyn squinted into the late afternoon light to see the commotion. A group of knights and squires rode against the flow along the edge of the road.

"Make haste! Make haste!" they repeated as they passed the long line of men. "Hurry your march; the king needs every man at the next town!"

Each man gave his horse a kick, increasing the column's pace to a trot. William felt behind him for his bow case and arrow bag to ensure that they remained strapped to his back. He turned and patted the bundle of twenty-four arrows that he had lashed to the back of his saddle. Hedyn shuddered when he remembered the sound of French quarrels buzzing by his ears.

The towers of Arques Castle began to appear above the trees far ahead. Hedyn's heart thumped so hard it seemed to rattle his ribcage as the Altarnon company rode off the road and into the broad field next to the castle. The curtain walls of the castle were arranged in an elongated egg shape about two hundred paces long, with the blunt end of the egg at the south. A square tower keep lay at the south where a bridge spanned the moat, accessed by a massive wooden gate. A barbican and smaller gate lay at the north end of the egg.

The king kept his men mounted and arrayed his entire army in plain sight around the castle. Every man knew to stop just outside of crossbow range. Hedyn surveyed the ground then looked behind him. The prosperous town of Arques lay deserted. Not a single Frenchman stirred. No French goats or cattle or horses grazed the fields. Two bridges spanned the confluence of three small rivers next to the town. Massive piles of large timbers blocked their use.

When he turned back, hundreds of Frenchmen appeared on the parapets of the castle. A crack of thunder and a burst of white smoke sent a gun stone the size of a pumpkin bounding across the field. Men ducked reflexively, and a few horses danced nervously, but no man moved from his post. The stone struck no one as it bounced and flew over the line of men. Hedyn heard it crash somewhere far behind in the town. The French had announced that the English were not welcome.

"William, such a nice town. Where are the people?" Hedyn asked.

William laughed. "This town has no walls. Apparently, the people took their animals and valuables and fled to the safety of the castle. They surely heard what happened at Harfleur and have expected our arrival for some time."

Hedyn nodded. The castle was not a large one. He tried to imagine several hundred frightened townspeople, with all of their livestock, crowded together within its walls.

To his right, Hedyn saw the king's banner and a tight knot of horsemen around it. The king held an impromptu council of war with his lieutenants near the moat bridge at the north end of the egg.

"Look yonder," William said to Hedyn and Denzel as he gestured toward the king. "King Henry knows he has not the time to besiege this castle and that it would be much too costly in lives to attack it. I wager he will be making an offer to the French commander."

Hedyn remembered the terror he felt when he helped to fill the moat at the Leure Gate. He did not want to repeat that nightmare. He prayed silently that William was right and that the king would launch no attack.

A brightly uniformed herald left the king's entourage and galloped forward under his banner to approach the castle gate. The whole army watched him wait patiently on the far side of the moat until a small door embedded in the massive castle gate opened tentatively. A man looked nervously in both directions then slowly stepped through the door. His clothing indicated wealth, but he wore no sword or armor—a merchant, Hedyn guessed. The man jumped and turned back to the door when it slammed loudly behind him. The English lines exploded in laughter. Even the anxious Hedyn managed a smile. The frightened Frenchman turned back to the herald, unsure of what to do or even if he would survive the encounter. The herald beckoned and the man approached within speaking distance. Hedyn could hear none of the conversation, but the wild gesturing by the Frenchman revealed that he did not receive Henry's message well. Having delivered his message from King Henry, the herald galloped back to the English lines. The Frenchman trudged back to the gate door and pounded for reentry. A delay in opening and another burst of frantic pounding brought about more laughter. When the door finally opened, the man pushed his way in as though a pack of hounds were on his heels.

The army waited silently in place. Even the horses grew bored. Hedyn's old mare began to crop the vegetation at her feet, but he held in her reins when she tried to move to fresher grass. He looked up when the gate door reopened. A knight and a finely dressed, rotund man wearing a wide gold chain and medallion were led out by the man who had first spoken with the herald. The knight looked defiant, but the fat man's eyes darted around nervously. The king's herald rode out to meet them.

"The lord of the castle and the mayor of the town," he heard William say.

The four men spoke for a few minutes before the herald returned to King Henry. A wave of cheering swept through Henry's entourage and spread both ways along the English line.

William saw the question on Hedyn's face. "The castle has capitulated," William said with a broad smile. A rush of relief washed through Hedyn. His prayer had been answered: none of his friends would die while storming this castle.  Later Hedyn learned that Henry did not threaten the inhabitants of the castle; he simply stated that no stone would be left upon another in Arques Town.  He would burn the town and tear down every building if the French did not un-block the bridges and let his army pass unmolested. With no French army nearby to rescue them, they would not sacrifice their homes and possessions for French honor.  The mayor also agreed to provide the English with wine and bread.

"The bread and wine does not go far when divided among six thousand hungry men," Denzel said as he drained the dregs from his cup. Hedyn silently agreed.  A meager chunk of bread the size of his fist and one cup of wine made up the boy's share.  The Altarnon men sat on the grass and watched as some of the townspeople toiled at removing the obstructions on the bridges.

"This is the kind of victory I prefer!" Sir John announced from his courser.  The archers came swiftly to their feet.  "We get fed, no one gets hurt, and we can go on our merry way!"  Squire John sat astride his horse next to his father.  He nodded to Hedyn.

"Pardon us, Sir John, we did not hear you approach," William offered.

"No matter.  Enjoy your rest.  We will camp here tonight.  The king reminds us of his edict that we will treat the people here as subjects of the Crown as long as they are cooperative and take no arms against us.  There will be no rummaging for valuables in these people's homes. We will march again in the morning."

Hedyn found a spot to sleep under a broad oak tree. The inside of his thighs was chafed and his arse hurt from long hours in the saddle, but he did not care.  He fell asleep that night, satisfied that it would be an easy march to Calais after all.

# CHAPTER NINETEEN

### Near Eu, France
### 12 October 1415

"Seventeen miles to Eu. That is the last town in Normandy," Sir John told them when they broke camp at Arques. The day was dry but overcast. The army packed its meager belongings and resumed the march at daybreak. Sir John, the squire, and the men-at-arms all rode together with the other knights at the head of their division, while the Altarnon men rode with other companies of bowmen.

"There he be! That's Sir Thomas Erpingham. He has been appointed by the king as commander of all the army's archers," William said to his men as they rode from Arques. An old man, dressed in fine armor with his mane of white hair uncovered, stood by the road watching the men pass. He held his bascinet helm with its heavy mail aventail draped over his arm. He was ancient, over fifty years old, but fit and every inch the soldier. Hedyn smiled when he recognized Sir Thomas as the white-haired knight who had shown concern when Roger fell ill by the trail at Harfleur.

The column snaked its way north along the Montivilliers Road through fields and woods and along hedgerows at a steady but tedious pace. Toward the end of the day, the column halted unexpectedly. Intervals between men and their companies disappeared and the men crowded in places, as always occurs when thousands of men suddenly lose motion on a march. Hedyn could see the towers of a castle peaking over the trees far in the distance to his right. "There must be trouble at the head of the column for us to have stopped so suddenly," said Denzel.

To the boy's right, a large field, newly plowed for winter wheat, stretched eastward into the distance. The field shared a chest-high hedgerow with the Montivilliers Road for two hundred paces. Woods bounded the field at the north and south. A small copse of trees lined the road on the left side.

An old farm track, just wide enough for two teams of oxen to pass, crossed the length of the field perpendicular to the Montivilliers Road. A break in the hedgerow provided access to the farm track.

Thundering hooves grabbed Hedyn's attention. A courier galloped up, its hooves slinging dirt clods with every stride. He reigned in his horse, which almost sat down with the sudden, sliding stop. Hedyn could see him talking excitedly to Thomas Erpingham and gesturing wildly down the farm track that cut through the hedgerow. The courier and his horse bolted again, just as fast, back in the direction from where they he had come.

Erpingham stood high in his saddle and commanded, "Archers, to the hedgerow. All others conceal yourselves in the woods with the horses!" Every archer within earshot began to dismount. Three hundred men swarmed behind the hedge.

"Lads, you heard Lord Erpingham," William announced. "Hedyn, you will hold our horses in yon wood," he said as he pointed across the road. And the archers placed the reins of their mounts into the boy's hands.

Hedyn started to complain, but a stern look from his ventenar kept him silent. He led the horses off the road to just inside the tree line. The weary mounts did not complain or falter but stood at rein's length, with their ears perked, sensing tension among the men. Since most of the summer leaves had fallen from the trees in the autumn weather, Hedyn had no trouble finding a vantage point to see what might occur. He peered out to see Lord Erpingham still sitting high on his courser.

"Lads, a body of French men-at-arms is approaching through yon field. They will appear at any time. You will remain down behind this hedgerow until I tell you to rise and shoot." The archers all crouched behind the earth bank and tangled shrubs of the hedgerow. Erpingham looked east across the field for a moment. "Your mark will be at one hundred paces," he called out.

No sooner had Erpingham finished his instructions, than Hedyn saw the French top a rise about four hundred paces away. The French, led by a resplendently armored knight astride a gigantic white charger, came on two abreast. With their visors up so they could search out the enemy, fifty or more men-at-arms armed with lances advanced at a trot. The archers waited grimly behind the hedgerow with arrows nocked on their strings and more arrows at hand. Hedyn had never seen his enemy in force and in the open before. They terrified and fascinated him at the same time. *Why doesn't Lord Erpingham give the order to shoot?*

Still they came, and Thomas Erpingham waited patiently, watching the enemy close the distance.

The armored French knights looked invincible. *What will I do if the French knights get past my archers?* Hedyn looked behind him for a route of escape. He decided he would drop the bridle reins and bolt if the French got to the hedgerow. Still Erpingham waited. *Why won't they shoot?* The lead knight's vivid red and gold surcoat designs were close enough for Hedyn to make out clearly from where he stood.

The French rode confidently, oblivious to the ambush. They rode straight toward Thomas Erpingham, sure of victory against a single English knight.

"Rise up!" Erpingham commanded without excitement. "Draw!" He continued calmly. "Loose!"

Hedyn had never seen so many men shoot at one time. As the archers muscled the cords to their ears, they almost seemed to squat as if lifting a heavy weight. When they loosed, the sudden release of the heavy bows pulled them forward a step or two. It reminded Hedyn of a dance—but this was a dance of death.

Three hundred bows twanged in unison, and three hundred arrows fluttered into the sky like a flock of murderous birds. Hedyn watched in wonder as they reached their apogee where the goose feathers disappeared into the grayness of the sky. They reappeared as they began their descent like a single deadly creature. Before the first arrows were halfway through their course, a second flight took wing. A third volley soon followed. The effect of the arrow storm was instantaneous.

Arrows zipped in to strike men and beasts alike. Many of the iron tips clanged on armor, but just as many made a sickening "thwack" as they bit into flesh. The head of the column crumpled in a mass of clanging armor, shrieking animals, and thrashing hooves. Dead and wounded men and horses littered the road. The white horse danced in terrified circles, screaming in pain and terror. His rider lay dying on the ground, but he still held the reins. As long as he stood, the beast drew attention and more arrows. The white courser finally went down on top of the knight who had ridden him to his death.

Rider-less horses galloped crazily in all directions with their reins and stirrups flapping on their necks and withers. One horse continued straight down the track and through the hedgerow. The archers parted their line and the horse disappeared into the woods, not to be seen again. The surviving French men-at-arms turned and galloped back the way from which they came, some riding, some running. It was the longest minute Hedyn had ever endured.

For a moment, a hush fell over the Montivilliers Road, every man in awe at the effect of the arrows. Several men started to push through the hedge to make their way to the carnage in the field.

"You, men! Stop there and return to your post. We have no time for plunder. There may be more of the enemy about," Thomas Erpingham called out, speaking to all of the men who could hear his voice. A low groan emitted from the archers.

Denzel pointed to the white charger which had finally gone still. "There must be a score of arrows sticking in that poor beast and half that many in its master."

"I'd wager it does not pay to announce yourself in such a fancy way when there are Englishmen about!" another archer chimed in. "A fine target indeed."

Hedyn realized that his hands trembled. One of the horses in the field tried to stand, fell back, and became still. A wounded man called out in French, but the boy could not understand him.

The column began to move again, more swiftly than before. As Hedyn reached the outskirts of the town of Eu, he saw the aftermath of the fight that had halted the column before the attack on his archers. A French knight and an English knight lay dead near one another, each impaled by the other's lance. Denzel pointed to a knot of horsemen who stood ahead by the side of the road. "There is Sir John, the squire, and Tregeagle. They are safe!"

William described the fight on the Montivilliers Road to Sir John and the squire. Jan Tregeagle showed no interest. He rode over to where Hedyn sat on his mare. "I heard that a boy fell from his horse and was run over by a cart during the march. Dead." Tregeagle whispered to Hedyn. "Now I am disappointed to find that it was not you." He silently mouthed the words, "I should have killed you," and laughed while he rode his horse slowly back to stand near Sir John. A chill went up Hedyn's spine. *He is making a game of tormenting me.* But Hedyn knew he could not reveal the man's cowardice. "Just a little pile of bones in the forest," kept ringing through his mind.

The garrison at Eu Castle surrendered under the same terms as Arques. Henry promised not to destroy the town for unmolested passage. The town also provided bread and wine, but there was little to share among six thousand Englishmen. Hedyn received none.

The Altarnon men sat around a small fire in the woods near Eu re-living the skirmish on the hedgerow over and over again. Each man's boast of how many arrows he put into the French grew with every telling. William said little, but smiled and laughed with the other men.

William ate the last spoonful of mushy peas from his wooden trencher. "Denzel, how much peas remain?" Most of their marching rations brought from Harfleur consisted of dried green peas. "Three days' worth. Almost enough to get us to Calais," Denzel answered.

"We will go on half rations tomorrow. The scanty bread and wine from this town helped us not. I would rather be cautious and finish the march a little hungry each day instead of chancing having nothing at all in our bellies when we reach Calais. The king will have to avoid fortified towns, and the smaller towns will be prepared for us now. We'll get no food from the French from now on. We go on half rations, at least until we cross the River Somme."

# CHAPTER TWENTY

**South of Corbie, France**
**17 October 1415**

The River Somme is not a long river. It flows a little more than one hundred and fifty miles through the chalk lands of northern France. Its water moves slowly through the gentle gradient that leads west to the British Sea without one waterfall or rapid. Broad marshes line the river for much of its length, leaving only a few places where it can be bridged or forded easily. The placid nature of its current provides its name. Somme comes from an old Celtic word meaning "tranquility."

While the Somme may be described as tranquil, its banks and the land that it drains have seldom deserved such a peaceful description. Armies have marched, fought, and pillaged through the valley of the Somme since armies first existed. Hedyn could not know it, but armies would continue to savage the peace along the Somme for another five hundred years after Henry marched his men to Calais.

The River Somme empties into a long, wide estuary before spilling into the British Sea. At low tide, a ford appears on the sandy flats. The ford at Blanche Taque, the most direct route to Calais, has been used since men lived in the valley. Even the Roman legions considered it an ancient ford. It was wide enough for twelve men to cross abreast and over a mile and a half long. In some places a man could keep his feet dry, in others he would be thigh-deep in brackish water. If he was halfway across when the sea returned, he would surely drown, for the water would flow far above his head.

Henry knew the history of this crossing place. His great-grandfather, Edward III, crossed his army here sixty years before as he marched to victory at the Battle of Crécy. The French knew their history too. On October 13th, the king's scouts found the ford blocked by an army of six thousand French men-at-arms and crossbowmen defended the crossing at Blanche Taque. King Henry turned his army east in a desperate search for an unguarded crossing. Crossing farther to the east would take the English away from the quickest course to their destination. Each step upriver was a step farther away from Calais and safety. The French force that blocked the crossing at Blanche Taque raced east also, paralleling the English on the opposite bank of the river.

It became a deadly game of cat and mouse. Every town and castle was on high alert. The English dashed to each potential crossing point, where Henry found the bridge destroyed and a large French force waiting for him on the north shore of the Somme. Attacking an equal-sized force in open terrain would be risky. Attacking the same force across a bridge or ford would be suicidal.

The French were not yet ready to challenge the English in open battle. They knew that each day would find their foe hungrier, more exhausted, and farther from refuge at Calais. A smaller force of French-mounted knights rode ahead of the English on the south side of the Somme, warning the inhabitants of each un-walled town to flee with their belongings and to burn any food or supplies that might help the English invaders. Unlike Arques and Eu, there were no more easy victories to enjoy. Henry's army began to feel the effects of the French "scorched earth" plan. Two days had passed since they should have been in Calais. The men grew hungry and dispirited.

Hedyn's stomach rumbled. His breakfast of a half ration of peas had long since disappeared. They were the last of the rations brought from Harfleur, but at least he had eaten something. Few of the other ventenars had the foresight to put their men on half rations as William had done. Those men had exhausted their food days before. They foraged on shriveled summer berries from the countryside and a few walnuts and hazelnuts, which were just starting to ripen and fall from the trees. The Altarnon men would now share the same hungry fate as the rest of the army.

"We turn off the road here," William remarked as the snaking column turned north onto a small trail. A faded wooden sign at the junction read *Corbie*. "I've not been here, but I know of this town. Corbie is a walled town and guards the last crossing on the Somme before the great bend in the river."

"We cannot get across here if the town is walled. Why would the king take us here?" one of the archers asked.

"I care not where he takes us as long as there are victuals there!" Denzel said. "If the king had put us on ships to Calais, we would not be in this fix," he added indignantly.

117

They rode on sullenly until the trail emerged from the trees into a large clearing. A tall, lone oak tree stood next to the road. The king and his entourage stood behind the tree talking, their pages holding the reins of grazing horses beyond.

A dead man hung from the lowest branch of the oak. He swiveled slowly in a slight breeze. Denzel slapped Hedyn on the arm to get his attention and pointed to the dangling corpse.

A squire stood beneath the dead man and repeated as the men rode by, so that every soldier would hear, "In disobedience to his sovereign's orders, this man stole a pyx from a church. In disobedience to his sovereign's orders, this man stole a pyx from a church. In disobedience to his sovereign's orders, this man stole a pyx from a church..."

Hedyn stared at the corpse. His hands were bound behind him and his head twisted at an unnatural angle. His eyes bulged from their sockets and the whites of the eyes were flaming red. His tongue was swollen to three times its normal size and protruded from between blue lips. The face was hideous, but the boy could not tear his gaze away. The dead, accusing eyes seemed to follow him as he rode slowly past.

"So now the king is murdering his own men just for filching some trinket from a stinking crapaud church!" Denzel hissed as he tugged at his beard nervously. Some of the other men mumbled their assent.

"Take care, friend," William said. "Your speech borders on treason. Think about this. This army is starving, and our fate is uncertain until we get to Calais and safety. The king can ill afford to have discipline break down in this army. If the men begin to drift off or straggle for plunder, we will lose what strength we have and will be at the mercy of the French." William stood in his stirrups so all of his men could hear him. "Do not fret about this now. Say a prayer for that man and his family. But keep your resolve. Stay alert and follow orders. That is the only way we will see Cornwall again."

The column came to a halt. The men moved to the side of the road and dismounted to wait for orders. Hedyn squatted to stretch the aches from the inside of his legs. Try as he might, he could not shake the image of the dead thief's bulging eyes and swollen tongue.

A large group of knights and nobles crowded around the king's standard behind the hanging oak. Denzel gestured to the group. "Something has changed. I wager our lord will be giving us new orders soon." Almost on cue, the throng of men around the king began to disperse. Within a few minutes, Sir John Trelawny approached his archers with Squire John.

"We will not force a crossing here at Corbie. But before we move on, each archer and boy will cut a stake. Find a suitable young oak or chestnut. Cut stakes as big around as a man's arm and six feet long. Sharpen it on both ends. I care not how you carry the ponderous things, but each man is to take a stake with him when we leave this place." Sir John turned to William. "Ventenar, how do we fare on rations? Is there anything left?"

"We fare not at all well, Sir John. The Harfleur rations are long eaten. We are at the mercy of the countryside like everyone else," William reported.

"Aye, make do then. When you go into the forest to cut your stakes, forage for what you can find."

When Sir John was out of earshot, Denzel complained, "So now we are to be foresters and cut timber, on empty bellies no less!"

* * *

Five thousand hungry and exhausted men spread out to find trees and cut their stakes. By the time the Altarnon men left the road and went into the woods, men were already felling trees all around them.

"Most of the trees are too large," William said over the ringing of hundreds of axes. *Whack, whack* —the woods were alive with the sound of ax heads biting into oak. "There will be nothing left for us to cut in these woods. We will have to scatter to find suitable trees. Gather back here after you cut your stake. Do not tarry. I know not how long it will be before we march again." The men scattered in every direction.

Hedyn followed William because he didn't know where else to search. They re-crossed the road and headed to a copse of wood nearer to Corbie. "Fewer men are going to this wood. We shall find our stakes here," the big archer said over his shoulder to Hedyn.

119

When they entered the woods, it seemed strangely quiet to Hedyn. The Corbie road was just visible through the forest. After dismounting, they tied their horses. William unlashed a hand ax from his saddle. He removed his bow case from his back and hesitated for a moment before leaning it against the tree where his horse stood tied. A few yards away stood a young elm. The archer grasped the trunk and measured its height with his eyes. After felling and trimming it, it would yield a sturdy stake six feet long and the size of a man's arm.

William looked around. "You know, I fear we are now at the head of the army. That is why no one else cuts their stake in this wood. I did not realize that we had strayed so far from the others. No mind, we shall cut this and soon be back with our mates." William bent to work with his ax. The big archer's attention was focused on the tree and away from the road.

A faint noise in the distance drew Hedyn's attention. Jingling and clacking of metal drifted in from the direction of Corbie. He looked at the road and strained to hear between the crashes of William's ax. Just as a bugle sounded, the boy saw flashes of color and brilliantly polished metal through the trees. Shouts and the thunder of hooves followed as a hundred knights and men-at-arms began charging down the road toward the English.

*We are cut off*! Hedyn thought. "William!" He cried out.

The ventenar had already stood straight and turned when the bugle sounded. A look of surprise and dread flashed across his face.

Two French knights slowed and stopped when they heard Hedyn's call of alarm. They turned and crashed into the woods. To the boy, they seemed like giants on their towering coursers. Both were fully armored, one brightly shining, the other in menacing-looking, blackened plate steel. The black night lowered a lance and shouted, "Archers! Tuez-les! Tuez-les!" the other knight drew a large sword. The knights dodged trees and branches as they urged their mounts into the wood.

The sudden noise and rush of men and beasts panicked the archers' horses. William's horse squealed urgently and struggled to free herself from her tied reins. William rushed to retrieve his bow, but it cracked loudly when the frantic mare backed into the tree where it leaned. Hedyn's old mare made no sound, just broke her ties and bolted away. Hedyn had never seen her move so fast.

Hedyn stood paralyzed. Sunlight filtering through the trees glinted on the point of the lance as the black knight leveled his weapon and bore down on him.

# CHAPTER TWENTY ONE

**Near Corbie, France**
**17 October 1415**

The French knights moved as swiftly as their horses could carry them among the trees. The war-horses, although well-trained, were used to open fields. The black knight's courser dodged a branch and threw his rider off balance. When the knight accidentally dipped the tip of his lance, the point struck a tree stump. The impact caused the knight to tumble to the ground with a clatter of armor.

Hedyn's head told him to run, but his feet remained rooted to the ground.

The shining knight's horse slowed and sidestepped as the fallen man struggled to regain his footing.

William grabbed Hedyn by his bow case and cried, "Quick, deep into the trees, boy. If we are to survive, we must go where their horses cannot follow!"

"Run! Follow me!" The two darted deeper into the woods, dodging trees, pursued by the shining knight and later by the black knight who rejoined the chase. Their shouts and the sound of their horses began to fall farther behind them. To Hedyn it seemed as if they ran forever.

Deep in the forest they came to a low marsh. The boggy ground sucked at their boots as they stomped into a tangle of underbrush and branches. Hedyn stopped, unable to run any farther. Bent double, with hands on his knees, he gulped precious air into his lungs. William turned and looked in the direction from which they had come. He placed his upright finger against his lips. "Shhh." He strained to hear movement. "Me thinks they no longer pursue. No sane man would bring horses into this bog. We will be safe here for a bit."

Hedyn dropped to the ground and sat against a tree. The soggy ground soaked through his hose and tunic bottom. William joined him but kept a wary eye. They sat in silence for a long while.

William broke the silence. "I have placed you in a dangerous spot, young Hedyn. I should have paid more mind to where we strayed. For that, I beg your forgiveness."

"You need no forgiveness. How could you know the French would sortie from the town?" Pointing to the hole in his helmet where the crossbow quarrel almost killed him, he added, "I would be dead at Harfleur if you had not thought to find this helm for me. Do you think it is safe now? Should we try to go back to our company?" he asked William.

"Nay. Not the way we came. The French sortie was small and our men would have repulsed them. But some of the enemy will remain between us and our army as spies and flankers." A sudden realization came to William's face. "Our young king is craftier than I credited him. Look hither." William brushed the leaves away to smooth the moist ground. With the point of his dagger he scratched a wavy line into the dirt. "This is the River Somme. Our army has been traveling on the south side, searching for a place to cross," William explained.

"Aye, and the French pursue us on the north side of the river and always reach each crossing point before we do. Pray tell why this makes our king crafty," Hedyn asked.

"Corbie lay at the base of the great northern bend of the river." William added a large hump to the line he had drawn in the dirt and stabbed the point of the dagger into the soil. "Henry only feigned a crossing here at Corbie. That drew together all of the French forces on the north side of the river to oppose his crossing. He plans to take his army overland straight east across the base of the great bend. The French, when they finally determine that there will be no crossing, will have to pursue following the river over the top of the bend and will have twice as far to travel. Our army will be on the other side of the bend and across the river before the French can oppose us."

"Will this scheme work?" Hedyn asked.

William smiled and nodded his head. "I dare say it will! If not, our army's only hope is to march all the way to the headwaters of the Somme to cross. By then we could all die of hunger. As for us, we will walk straight east with the sun to our back until dark, then continue with the sun on our face in the morn. We will catch up with the army tomorrow or the next day."

* * *

William raised his arm, a silent signal to stop, as they came to the edge of a field. He held an arrow ready on Hedyn's bow because his own lay broken where his horse had trampled it when the knights attacked. Before they set out to catch up with their friends, the boy had offered his bow to William. "Here, you must use this to protect us. I can hardly draw it myself anyway," he had explained.

The field was long but narrow. As with so many fields before, he scanned every direction to ensure that no Frenchmen, soldiers, or peasants were about.

"Where are all the people? No one works the fields," Hedyn asked.

"Hiding somewhere at a manor or castle, maybe even deep in the forest. They know our army is on the march," William explained.

Only when the big archer was certain that no one watched, they dashed to a hedgerow and followed it to the next copse of woods.

Eastward, always eastward, they trudged, making their way cautiously across the hostile countryside. Several times during the day they heard French voices in the distance. This confirmed William's fear that enemy scouts were keeping watch over the English advance. Danger still lay between them and their friends.

The last of the sun's western rays filtered through the trees and a cold breeze drifting in from the north hinted of rain. Sharp pains of hunger squeezed at Hedyn's guts. He was lightheaded, and the muscles in his weary legs screamed for him to rest. A dog barked far to their north, and the pair stopped to try to pinpoint the direction of the danger. William looked down at the boy, just then realizing how exhausted he appeared.

"You look pitiful, boy. We shall go just a bit farther to make certain yonder dog cannot get our scent. Then we shall stop for the night."

A short time later, they came to the edge of a small clearing.  The smell of pigs and charred wood hung in the air.  The waning autumn twilight barely revealed a small waddle-and-dob cottage on the opposite side of the glen.  A few sparks swirled up into the gathering dark from the smoke hole in the roof.  A dim oil lamp inside cast a few pitiful points of light from around the rude plank door.  The humble cottage reminded Hedyn of his own, and a sudden rush of homesickness flooded through him.

"Cotters," William said in a low voice.  "Charcoal burners, I'd wager."  Hedyn knew that in his world, cotters were the only folk lower than villeins, lower than himself.  A man's angry cursing burst from the cottage.  William and Hedyn instinctively ducked behind a tree.  The cursing mingled with the crying and pleading of girls' voices, little girls.  Hedyn could not understand the French tongue, but William listened intently.  He smiled and chuckled softly to himself.

"The little girls have been told to take a tub of malt, left over from making ale, out to the pig sty.  They do not want to go out into the dark because the savage islanders will kill them and eat them."

Hedyn looked at him quizzically.

"We are the savage islanders, boy.  It is the English they fear!" William whispered.  Hedyn blinked and nodded.

"The father has tired of their stalling and insists they take the tub to the pigs."  Just as William finished the translation, the door opened a crack and two tiny silhouetted figures slipped out, struggling with a heavy tub between them.  The door closed, and they became almost invisible.

Excited whispers drifted on the light breeze.  William cocked his head to better hear the girls.  "Ha, they say they are too afraid to take the tub all the way out to the pig sty.  They will leave it where they stand and take the beating their father will give them in the morn," William explained in a low voice. He added, "We shall have our supper."

A few minutes later, shafts of light escaped from the open door and the little silhouettes slipped back inside the cottage.

It seemed like forever as Hedyn waited for William to fetch the tub and bring it safely back to the woods.

Malted barley for making ale was not intended to be eaten by people. The grain was not winnowed to remove the chaff and husks. The old ale malt had soured and made poor porridge, but they did not care. They pushed the sticky gruel into their mouths by the dirty handful. After a time their urgency to eat abated, and they began to dip their fingers into the tub with more delicacy.

Hedyn's face, hands, and chest became smeared with a slowly hardening mess, but that too mattered little to him. Barley husks stuck to the roof of his mouth like little bits of soggy paper. It was the first real meal he had enjoyed in days. All he cared about was that his starving belly no longer cried out for food.

* * *

Hedyn belched and said, "I never thought pigs' food could taste so good!" William leaned his back against a tree. "I have eaten worse and believed myself favored to have had it," he said with a yawn.

Hedyn sat and hugged his knees to ward off the gathering cold. "William, the cotter will beat his little girls when he finds the tub missing in the morn." Hedyn thought of his sister Tressa, not much older than the French girls who were too afraid of the English to take the tub into the dark.

"I wager he will," William said with a sigh. "Does your father beat you, Hedyn?" he asked.

'My tas whips me sometimes when I disobey or neglect my work, but no more than any other boy in Altarnon, I suppose."

The night grew full and dark, and Hedyn could only see only an occasional glint of moonlight reflecting from William's eyes.

"My Father would beat me with his staff. My mother too, on occasion. Sometimes I never learned why. That ceased when I was sent to the monastery to live."

"You were a monk!" Hedyn exclaimed.

"Yes, I was a Benedictine monk at Saint Nicholas Priory in Exeter."

"A monk! Roger and I often speculated how you could be so wise and so learned! How did you come to choose to be a monk, and why are you no longer at an abbey?"

"I have already revealed too much to you, but sometimes it does a man good to tell his secrets. I consider you a friend. Can I trust your discretion?"

Hedyn nodded.

The big archer sighed heavily and adjusted his back against the oak tree.

"I did not choose to go to Saint Nicholas. My father was a freeman tenant on the priory land. My grandparents were villeins, but they became free during the Great Mortality. When their lord died, they simply walked away from the manor and ended up in Devonshire where my father was born."

"Villeins, like me?" Hedyn asked.

"Aye. My father was a villein's son too. He had only a quarter of a hide of land--only big enough to grow sufficient grain to pay his rents and feed his family. And it was a big family. There were four girls still alive when I left and three boys, me being the youngest. My parents had no hope of getting more land for three boys when we came of age, and there were no craftsmen nearby to seek an apprenticeship. There was no future for me. I was considered a burden--just another mouth to feed.

In my ninth year, my father and mother took me to Saint Nicholas. They had me wait outside the door while they bargained with the abbot. They didn't know that I could hear every word. My father made an impassioned speech and explained that he had a vision from God. He longed to honor God by offering his favorite son for service to the church. I'm certain the abbot saw through my worthless father's false speech, but I suppose he pitied me. I listened to them bargain back and forth for some time before they settled on the price of one heifer, ten pigs, a tithe of grain for five harvests, and ten silver pennies. The price is still burned in my mind."

Hedyn gasped. "Your tas sold you!"

"Nay, that is what they PAID to the priory to get rid of me," William said with a sigh. "As I said, the abbot must have had pity that

127

day, because the families of most novices paid much more to get their child into an abbey or priory."

Hedyn sat stunned. He did not know what to say.

"I grieved at first. I missed my brothers and sisters. But in time, I embraced being a novice monk and all that it meant. For the first time I had plenty to eat and I was never punished unless I deserved it. And I served God, after all. Or, so I thought. I absorbed everything taught to me. When they found that I had an aptitude for reading and writing, they trained me to be a scribe. By the time I took my vows, I was also the librarian."

"So that is how you came to learn to read," Hedyn said.

"Oh, much more than read! I learned Latin and Greek and a host of other languages. The priory library was a massive one—over two hundred books and growing. I read them all, many times over. We would borrow books from other monasteries and transcribe them for our library. We would also copy our books to be sold to wealthy patrons. But most importantly, I learned to think for myself. I learned to examine everything with a critical eye—to analyze everything closely for truth and consistency." The archer paused and said, "I suppose that was my undoing."

Hedyn came to his knees. "William, how could becoming wiser be your undoing?" he asked urgently.

"Of all the reading and transcribing I performed, most was with the Holy Scriptures. I learned them better than many Bishops or Cardinals. The more I learned, the more I realized that what the Church taught and practiced was full of half-truths, fabrication, and superstition. Much of it had no basis in the word of God. Most profoundly, I learned that the Bible teaches us that all men, no matter how lowly, can enjoy the same close relation to the Savior. We need no other men or earthly institutions to act as intermediaries for us."

William became quiet for a moment and Hedyn sensed that he was drifting away in thought. Hedyn gave a gentle prod. "William, how were you undone?"

The big archer sighed and continued. "From time to time I traveled to other monasteries to transcribe books in those collections. Completing one book often took weeks or even months. On one such trip, I met a Cistercian monk who shared much of my interest in reading and philosophy. He confided in me that he secretly followed the teachings of John Wycliffe. I was aghast! My superiors always spoke of Wycliffe as a great heretic and agent of the devil and that his Lollard followers were just as evil. But this monk showed me a copy of Wycliffe's writings. I found that what Wycliffe taught was what I had already come to believe! I grew very excited to learn that others held the same views. I made a secret copy of Wycliffe's book during my stay. Wycliffe also supported translating the Bible into English so the common people could read it for themselves and better understand God's will. Wycliffe and the Lollards were not agents of the devil; they were simply a threat to the ungodly men who ruled the Church."

"But William," Hedyn asked, "is that not what our priests and monks are for, to explain to us what the scriptures say and to tell us what God would have us do? They offer prayers for ordinary people because God will hear their prayers much better."

"That is exactly Wycliffe's dissent with the Church, and mine. The Church forbids the translation of the Bible into English. They want to keep that knowledge and power in the hands of the priests and monks. I suspect they fear the day when God's people come to know what the Scriptures truly say."

Hedyn sat back down. He remained silent, trying hard to understand what William had explained.

"Over time, I began to accept what I had been denying to myself for several years. I became more and more disillusioned—not with God, but with the Church. The Church and what it practices is of men, not of God. My disillusionment culminated with news of Lollards being burned at the stake as heretics. Scores of men and women, who truly know Christ as their savior, have been martyred in this way by men who profess to be God's representatives on Earth."

Hedyn sat up again. "So that is why you left the priory and became an archer," he said.

William's eyes twinkled in the moonlight as he shifted his weight against the tree. "That came later. A young villein couple came to the priory with a child burning of fever. I happened to be the first to greet them at the gate. They had a handful of copper farthings and wanted to give every coin they owned for the monks to pray for their child. It made me think of the story in the Gospel of Mark about the widow who gave two tiny coins, all that she had, as an offering to God.

I praised them for their faith in God to heal their child and told them to keep their money and buy nourishing food for their babe—that I would pray earnestly for them without the need for payment. Further, I told them that their prayers, if given in earnest, would be heard by Christ as well as if offered by the Pope himself. They left puzzled, but the prayers were already on their lips even as they left the priory grounds.

When I turned to go back to the scriptorium, I found Brother Ralph, the circuitor, watching me. The circuitor is the monk in charge of keeping discipline. Brother Ralph berated me for refusing the money, but he was most aghast at my suggestions that the prayers of a villein are just as potent as those of the Pope. He accused me of blasphemy and took me straight to Brother Andrew, the abbot. Brother Andrew was a new abbot. He was ambitious and zealous and longed to find favor with Bishop Edmond in Exeter. I defied Brother Andrew and reaffirmed my belief that all men are equal in God's eyes and that the Priory and Church should not continue to grow fat on the money and labor of the poor. To this day, I do not know whether it was sinful pride which spurred on my speech or a true desire to do God's will. While we were discussing this, rather loudly I might add, Brother Ralph went through my belongings and found my Wycliffe book—and something else much more damning. He found a copy of the four gospels that I had translated into English."

"But William, why is having a Bible damning?" Hedyn asked.

"It was an English Bible, young Hedyn. To translate the Bible into English is considered heresy by the Church. They burn heretics. Even our King Henry supports the Church's authority in burning heretics."

William continued, "Brother Andrew told me that he would take me to Bishop Edmond on the morrow. There I was to confess my sins, beg forgiveness, and swear penitence. He sent me to the dorter, the place where the monks sleep. I was to stay there until the morn and attend none of the services with the other monks but remain in constant prayer. When the other brothers went to Matins for prayer, I slipped out of the priory with a small sack that held all that I owned. I knew that I could not bring myself to ask for forgiveness or seek penitence from

130

Bishop Edmond. And, unless I renounced my beliefs, he would be forced to try and burn me according to the laws of the Church. I had a simple choice—either flee or burn."

"So you ran away and became an archer!" Hedyn exclaimed. "And it was your abbot and Brother Ralph who pursued you in Plymouth!" Hedyn said in sudden realization.

"Aye. That was Brother Andrew and Brother Ralph. I was hoping that five years away would make it safe to return to Devonshire. I was mistaken. Even after all this time, I still sometimes think that I betrayed my Lord for fleeing. I feel like the apostle Peter when he denied Christ three times in Jerusalem. Mayhap I should have faced the bishop and been martyred as the others."

"William, you didn't deny Christ. Doing his will as you saw it is what brought your troubles! You once told me that the only important thing is each man's trust in Christ and his own salvation. Does not God know your heart—a heart that is true? Would burning have made your heart any truer?"

William remained silent for a moment and then said, "You are wise beyond your age, young Hedyn. My heart is true for my Lord. That has not changed and never will, wherever he might lead me."

They talked quietly, long into the night. William recounted to Hedyn how he fled Devonshire, changed his name, and served a series of lords as a soldier. His skill as an archer and a leader improved with each campaign. But his secret made him cautious about what he said around other men, and he always remained an outsider.

"Hedyn, you are the first person who I have been able to call a friend since I left Saint Nicholas," he confided.

As Hedyn curled up and began to drift off to sleep, he heard William lift the malt tub, leave the trees, and carry it quietly across the glen to the pig sty. The little French girls would receive no beating when the morning came.

# CHAPTER TWENTY TWO

**Béthencourt-sur-Somme, France**
**18 October 1415**

Warm breath and kisses. Hedyn felt the light touch of his mamm's lips. He could see her in his slumber, stroking his hair and kissing him. Then slobber. Wet, thick slobber dropped to his cheek. Hedyn popped open his eyes to see enormous yellow teeth inches from his face. He shrieked and rolled away. William was on his feet in a flash, his short sword drawn and ready. Hedyn's old palfrey stood looking at him and William suspiciously. After a moment of silence they both hooted with laughter.

"Ha, I cannot believe my eyes! Your old horse has found you! She licks the malt from your face," William exclaimed.

The horse stood and looked at them as though expecting something. Her saddle was loose and hung lopsided from her back. Sticks and leaves were wedged in her leather tack. Leather reins hung broken from her bridle, snapped from when she fled the French attack at Corbie.

Hedyn stepped lightly forward and took her by the iron bit. "I didn't think I'd ever see you again, girl." The horse shifted weight on her hooves and nuzzled the boy in his neck. She took another long, wet lick of dried malt from his tunic shoulder. "William, I have never named my palfrey, but I shall do so now," Hedyn announced.

"And what would her name be?" William asked.

"I wanted to call her *Dyowl* back when she bit and kicked me. But now she has found us and will take us back to our friends. I will call her *El*."

William laughed. "In Cornish, *dyowl* is 'devil' and *el* is 'angel.' I suppose that is most fitting."

The old horse carried them steadily across open fields with Hedyn sitting behind William in the saddle. In the forest they slowed, and El picked her way carefully between giant oaks and towering elms. They made good time, always traveling east. At dusk they came to a muddy road churned by thousands of feet and hooves. A six-foot-long oak stake lay abandoned by the road.

"Look, William." Hedyn pointed to the ground. "Our army has passed this way and we surely cannot be far behind."

"Aye, but we will not catch them this day. It will be full dark soon and it will be unsafe to follow. We'll spend one more night in the woods. In the morn we shall catch them."

Before daybreak, Hedyn saddled El and they were riding east. El had eaten her fill of grass, but William and Hedyn had to be satisfied with a handful of hazelnuts scavenged from a hedgerow.

William's prediction came true. An hour after sunup they heard voices from up the narrow road. William slowed El and cocked his head to better hear. "English," he said with a grin. He urged El into a cantor and rounded a bend in the road to find a company of archers merrily disassembling a villein's cottage.

"Ho there!" William cried out.

Several of the men turned and drew swords but relaxed after seeing the pair.

"Who's this?" a tall thin man stepped forward. A tangle of flaming red hair escaped in all directions from his dirty linen coif. "What is your business?"

A bone-thin woman with wild black hair pulled another slat of wood from the cottage. She blew a tuft of hair from her cockeyed face and said, "They ain't supposed to be no Englishmen behind us." The woman gestured toward Hedyn, but she seemed to look in a different direction.

"My name is William Whitwell. I am ventenar of Sir John Trelawny's company. We became separated at Corbie."

"I am ventenar of this useless crew." The red-haired man motioned to the bedraggled men who gathered around. "Corbie. That was two days back! We are about to cross the river now. Some of the lads have already forded on foot and are guarding the other side. Everyone else has been sent out to find wood and stones to repair the causeway that leads across a swamp to the river." He laughed, "There won't be many crapaud houses left by the time we are done here!"

Hedyn imagined some poor villein family hiding in the woods that would have no home to return to.

William let out a whoop. "So Henry's scheme worked! We have found a crossing before the French arrived to stop us."

"I know nothing about a scheme," the red-headed man said. "But we have two crossings. One is just up the road for the baggage train, and the other is another mile up the river at some place called Voyennes. The men-at-arms and most of the archers will cross there. We shall all be across the Somme and on our way to Calais before night falls!"

\* \* \*

At mid-afternoon, men, horses, and carts began headed for the causeway. Hedyn heard no signal, but the orchestrated movement of men and animals signaled to him and William that the repairs were finished and it was time for crossing the Somme.

Hedyn could feel a change in the moods of the men around him. In the days before there was despair. Today there was hope. Expectation hung in the air like a scent on the breeze that everyone could detect. Some men laughed and smiled, others stood in their stirrups and strained to see ahead of them.

Knights in the king's livery stood along the way, battered helmets tucked under their arms, directing and reassuring the men. "No need to rush or press in. Every man shall cross safely. Plenty of room for three horses abreast. Move up, no need to press in." A less-disciplined army may have panicked and rushed the crossing in a chaos of tangled men, horses, and carts.

William urged El forward slowly as the queue formed near the causeway, carts and wagons alternating with horses and riders at the direction of the knights. El wedged between two packhorses piled high with sheaves of arrows, both led by boys younger than Hedyn.

"They'll be eats a plenty when we gets to Calais," one of the boys said jubilantly. Hedyn could not tell the scroungy waifs apart. *Must be brothers*, he thought.

"Aye, and I'll have me own pigeon pie to eat all by me self!" the other boy announced. The boys bantered back and forth about what and how much they would eat. Hedyn's belly rumbled with the thought of food. Any food.

Causeway was a generous title for the mud, rocks, and wooden track that they traversed through the marsh. It was little more than a slightly elevated road that kept them from sinking into the swampy morass. Over a mile they traveled, until the causeway blended into the banks of the river. Hedyn heard faint cheers far up ahead. William smiled. "Me thinks men have crossed and are joyous for it!"

The water flowed shallow at the ford at Béthencourt, yet El eyed the water nervously. William gave the old mare his heels, and she stepped tentatively into the current. Water flowed up to her belly, but she did not falter even under the load of a big man and small boy. El struggled up the mud bank on the opposite shore and shook the water from her coat, almost throwing William and Hedyn from the saddle. Hedyn held on and laughed - the first real laugh he remembered for weeks.

William let out a sigh. "We are across, and God may have mercy on us yet!" He turned El east toward the other crossing at Voyennes.

"Any sign of the French?" William called out to some archers who lounged by the trail.

"Only a few cowards who stay out of bow range. They only spy on us to keep account of what we do," one of the men responded. Another added, "We did catch one who was napping. He says there are thirty five thousand men at Rouen who will be coming soon to kill us all."

# CHAPTER TWENTY THREE

**Near Péronne, France**
**21 October 1415**

Denzel Crocker rode beside William Whitwell as the English army moved cautiously west on the Calais Road. Hedyn and Father Stephen rode just behind them. "I didn't like being ventenar anyway. Too much work, not enough time for myself. I was very happy to see you and the boy ride up after the crossing. But Jan Tregeagle didn't seem too happy to see the two of you. Especially Hedyn. What does that lick-finger have against the lad?"

Father Stephen added, "Yes, we had given both of you up for dead. I was already rehearsing what I would tell poor Jago about his son when we returned to Altarnon." Hedyn came out of a near slumber when he heard his and his father's names. He knew exactly why Tregeagle hated him but said nothing in answer to Denzel's question.

Hedyn was, as most of the army, exhausted from constant movement and lack of food. He still marveled that he could find some rest while sitting astride his moving horse. El plodded on, following the others without instructions from her rider. Once he almost fell from her when she stopped suddenly, but he soon found that he could remain just inside of consciousness and rest while remaining clinched to his saddle.

The joy and merriment they had seen the night of the crossing slowly evaporated during the following days as the men remembered their hunger. Hedyn mentioned this to William, who replied, "Aye, but a man can abide hunger much easier if he has hope. Hope returned when we forded that river."

A half-hearted sortie by a small French force from Péronne broke the monotony of the ride earlier in the day. The French knights lost resolve when they neared the English column. Hedyn watched, relieved when they slunk back to the protection of their walls. No one pursued, either too exhausted or too intent to continue the march to Calais.

The column slowed and conversation among the men ceased suddenly. Hedyn shook the sleep from his head. At first he could not see what could be the matter, and then he noticed that all eyes were on the ground. One of the Altarnon archers crossed himself. The road beneath them and as far as he could see ahead was churned by the hooves and feet of tens of thousands of men and horses, crossing the Calais road at right angles.

"Well, the tracks tell us that the French are finally on the move from Rouen," said William solemnly. A pall of foreboding fell upon the archers. Hedyn looked at the road behind him and compared its width to the track where the French crossed the road. The width of the rutted tracks revealed that the French army was so large the road could not contain them, so their knights and men-at-arms had spread their column over the fields on either side. The rutted and churned path was three times wider than that of the English.

"Christ's bones! They crossed our path here; does that mean that the crapauds are ahead of us now?" Denzel asked.

"Aye, I fear so. They will travel ahead and block the road to Calais. They will choose the ground for a fight. Somewhere up ahead they will be waiting. And by the looks of these tracks, they will greatly outnumber us," William explained as he stretched in the saddle to see farther ahead.

"By the bowels of the saints!" Denzel complained. "If King Henry had taken us to Calais by shipping, we would not be in this trouble!"

"Denzel Croker, you have a useless talent foretelling the past. Please hold your tongue unless you can foretell the future as well," William commanded.

Denzel started to protest but remained silent.

Father Stephen clasped his hands and raised his eyes toward heaven. "In his goodness, may God have pity on us and turn from us the violence of the French!"

"We are not beaten yet, priest. Say your prayers, as all of us should, but we are not yet beaten. Don't forget what our grandfathers did at Crécy and Portieres," William said with confidence.

Some of the men nodded agreement before the column resumed the march up the Calais Road.

Even Hedyn knew that there would be violence. It could not be avoided. The French would not let them pass to Calais without a fight.

This would not be like the skirmishes that he had seen on the march. This would be a death struggle, one army against the other in open combat. One of those armies was exhausted and starving. The other was rested, well-fed, and in great numbers. The question was, would any of them survive to reach Calais and see home again?

# CHAPTER TWENTY FOUR

## Maisoncelle, France
## 24 October 1415

Hundreds of campfires glimmered in the darkness. French campfires. As Hedyn watched them, it seemed that all the stars in the cloud-masked sky had fallen instead to earth to array their constellations. Sparks swirled skyward from the larger of the blazes. Music, laughter, and a general hum of thousands of voices drifted between the French lines and the little village of Maisoncelle, where the English army encamped.

The two armies had ridden parallel with one another ten miles apart for the previous three days. Each day Hedyn expected the French to attack. Instead, the English trudged on to Calais, growing weaker with each hour. Finally, on this day, they found the French drawn up for battle, straddling their path to Calais and safety.

King Henry deployed his weary army to meet a French attack. But none came. The men stood with swords and bows ready. Hedyn gathered sheaves of arrows, ready at hand to issue to his archers. After an hour William said, "Unstring bows, lads. We don't want the wood to follow the strings." He looked up at the gray sky. "It looks like rain, so keep your bow cords dry." The men were nervous and anxious as they watched the French across the field. Hunger gnawed at their bellies as the first drops of scattered rain fell among them. The archers stuffed their precious bow strings under helmets and into leather belt pouches. A bow with a wet string has no power.

The French commanders chose their ground wisely. The Calais road passed through a large wheat field a half mile wide. Forest framed the field on both sides, with the Village of Tramecourt to the east. Agincourt Castle towered above the trees in the forest to the west. Maisoncelle stood at the south end of the wheat field. The three villages of Agincourt, Tramecourt, and Maisoncelle formed a deadly triangle, where the armies prepared for the battle that morning would surely bring.

As darkness began to fall and rain began to come, King Henry had his men stand down. There would be no French attack on that day.

Now Hedyn sat huddled under a tree and watched the French campfires. He shivered as a new icy stream of rain found its way under his blanket and trickled down his back. Five thousand archers found scant shelter from the rain and cold under the trees and hedges of Maisoncelle. The king and his nobles remained snug and dry in the collection of tiny cottages in the village.

Henry gave strict orders. There would be no music or loud voices in the English camp. The sentries needed to have keen ears in case the French should launch a night attack. No fires blazed for the archers. All of the dry wood burned in the fire pits of the cottages.

Hedyn sat with his back to the big elm tree that half of the Altarnon men shared with him. *Will this night ever end!* He watched the French fires twinkle as another burst of distant laughter drifted over from the French camp. Far into the night, exhaustion finally overcame the boy and he slipped into a fitful sleep. Still the rain came, and the great wheat field in the triangle between Maisoncelle, Agincourt, and Tramecourt became a sea of black mud.

* * *

A tap to Hedyn's head brought him from a dreamless sleep. William moved quietly in the early morning darkness rousing his archers. "Up lads, up," He whispered. "Gather your weapons and your stakes. We will be moving soon. Our company will fight with the king's division this day!" Hedyn looked around. There was no sign of the new sun on the eastern horizon, but a dim moon behind thinning clouds cast an eerie pall over the landscape.

Men moved quietly all around him. Some moaned. Knees popped and backs creaked as the men unfolded from a miserable night on the ground, but Hedyn heard none of the complaints that soldiers so often make. The gravity of the situation quelled the normal banter of the men. Each man knew what came with the light and what he must endure.

A flurry of harsh words interrupted the calm. Hedyn jerked his head around to see two figures in the dim moonlight. A soft glint of light from the taller of the two revealed that they were in armor. "You will do this thing!" the taller of the two said. It was Sir John and Squire

140

John. "You will remain here and guard the baggage train with the other sick men!"

"But Father!" the Squire exclaimed.

"Silence! And do as I bid!" Sir John commanded. Hedyn watched his friend storm off until his form was hidden in the moon shadows of the trees. Hedyn was pleased. *He will be out of harm's way,* he thought. *Unlike I, who will be standing with my archers against the French.*

William came and stood by Hedyn's side. "If I had a son and an honorable way to protect him, I would do the same as Sir John. A small group of unwell men-at-arms and archers will remain here and guard the baggage train. Squire John will be among them. He is noble boy, and this will sting him; but he is still weak from his sickness."

"Aye, and I am happy for it," Hedyn said. "Mayhap he will make it back home, even if we do not."

William handed Hedyn a blanket. "Is your horse tied well with the other palfreys?" he asked. "Aye, Ventenar. El is tied fast with the others," Hedyn answered.

"Good. All the horses will remain here. Each archer will carry one sheave of arrows with him. You are to bundle as many sheaves as you can in this blanket and carry them with us when we go. Make haste. It will be soon."

As the little band of Cornish archers marched away from Maisoncelle for their place in the line of battle, Hedyn shifted the burden of arrows that he carried on his back and looked behind him. A faint smear of orange in the eastern sky announced the arrival of the new sun. He could just make out Squire John standing alone, watching as they marched away.

* * *

Before the first rays of sun filtered through the clouds, King Henry's army was arrayed across the sodden wheat field. The king's division of three hundred men-at-arms stood in the middle of the field, formed up in two lines.

Two hundred archers anchored and protected the flanks of the king's division on either side. To the left and next in line were another three hundred men-at-arms. Three hundred more formed in line to the right. And finally, all the remaining archers were divided between the left and right of the army. Over two thousand bowmen formed a staggered line, five men deep, on each flank of the army. An unbroken line of Englishmen stretched across the muddy field and into the protection of the woods at either side.

The Altarnon men were honored by assignment to the archer contingent posted to the left of the king's division. It was a high honor, but this honor could be fraught with peril. As the first rays of the sun struggled to pierce the cloudy sky, the king's royal standard and the banners of a score of noblemen added a bit of color to an otherwise dismal landscape.

Few eyes were on the king. A thousand paces across the wheat field, the French army assembled. The French were also in three divisions, but to Hedyn's inexperienced eyes, it looked like a solid mass of men. Instead of side by side in line, the French divisions were one behind the other, and each of the three was much larger than the whole of the English army. Eight thousand men-at-arms and knights and four thousand crossbowmen of the first division crowded together across the field from wood to wood. Two similar divisions stood behind the first, ready to add their weight to the attack. Even in the dim morning light, the Frenchmen's armor was bright and polished, and their surcoats were clean and colorful. Hedyn could see the stark contrast between the fresh French troops and the bedraggled Englishmen in rusty plate steel and mud-matted mail. Most of the archers were barefoot, their boots destroyed by the hard march from Harfleur. They continued to battle persistent diarrhea, and many wore no britches despite the chilled air.

The long stakes that the men cut in faraway Corbie now came into play. The archer companies arrayed themselves in staggered lines five deep and used mauls and sledge hammers to drive their stakes into the muddy ground at an angle with the points waist-high. They could pierce the breast of any French horse that might gallop into the midst of the archers.

"Why do they not attack?" Denzel asked.

"They are in no hurry. They grow stronger with each minute and know that we grow weaker. They hope we will attack so they can make swift work of us. If the king has half a brain, he will provoke them to attack. That is our only chance." William explained.

They waited as the morning sun struggled and finally pierced the clouds. No French attack came. To Hedyn, it seemed an eternity.

King Henry appeared before the army on a little gray horse. He rode up and down the line, stopping here and there to encourage his men. The king seemed to glow in the morning light. His was the only polished armor in the whole of the English ranks. He wore a golden crown around his bascinet helmet that added a flash of yellow to the silver of his armor. His foes would have no difficulty finding him in the line of battle. His little horse pranced and danced impatiently in little circles when the king stopped to talk in front of Hedyn's part of the line. Henry was a young man, full of fire and confidence.

From where Hedyn stood at the back of the line, he could only make out snippets of what his king said. ". . . return to England covered in glory. . .band of brothers. . .the sovereign honor of England and your king." But every man heard his last sentence: "The French have boasted that they will cut two fingers from the right hand of every archer!" From somewhere in the line a man cried out, "Sire, we pray to God that he may grant you long life and victory over our enemies!" A great cheer rose up from the entire line. Hedyn had never felt so alive and so inspired. For a moment he forgot his hunger and his fear.

King Henry returned to the center of the line and sent his horse to the rear. All of his men would fight on foot. He was no exception. A swift change came over the army. The raucous cheers faded and transformed into resignation and reverence. Almost on cue, the army, to a man, went to its knees. Hedyn hesitated because he did not understand what his comrades were doing. He followed and watched as the men around him took a pinch of the black mud at their knees and placed it into their mouths. Some did so with bowed heads, others with head high and eyes on the heavens. He followed the example, not understanding what he did. He scrunched his eyes at the sour, earthy taste and swallowed.

The men stood. Some muttered prayers to themselves. Other raised muddy hands to the sky, entreating God for mercy in battle or to receive them into heaven should they fall. William was no different. He prayed silently and then turned to see the questions on Hedyn's face. "The men eat a morsel of earth as an act of humility, as they expect that they will return to that same earth before this day ends," he said without emotion.

The solemnity of the moment faded as word passed down the line. "Pull up your stakes. Prepare to move forward! Make haste!" Each man wrenched his stake from the black soil. Hedyn gathered all his sheaves of arrows and wrapped them in his blanket. Somewhere from the middle of the line a voice called out "In the name of Almighty God and Saint George!"

Trumpets sounded and the Englishmen advanced in line, dragging weary feet through the thick muck, each step taking them closer to the French. On they went—one hundred, two hundred, five hundred paces. Slow and steady they advanced, the line straight and intact, the flanks remaining anchored in the woods.

Three hundred paces from the French line, just inside bow range, a trumpet sounded and the march halted. The archers urgently went to work pounding their protective stakes back into the ground. The men had to turn backs to the enemy to accomplish this task. William constantly turned back to see the French response. "I can't believe it! They do not come when we are most vulnerable. They stand and watch us!" he said.

"More arrows, boy!" one of the Altarnon archers demanded as he stuck each of the twenty four arrows he already possessed into the ground at his feet. William nodded and Hedyn dropped another sheave of arrows at the feet of each of his comrades. They stood ready behind their stakes, bows strung, arrows at easy reach, and one arrow nocked and prepared to shoot.

Finally some movement in the French ranks. The men stiffened in anticipation, but to the surprise of all, the enemy crossbowmen were hustled to the rear of the line and replaced by more knights and men-at-arms. William shook his head in confusion. "What do they do? This makes no sense." Just then, a large gonne spouted smoke and flame from somewhere in the French line. *Ka-booooom*! The gun stone struck the earth halfway to the English line and sent a shower of mud in all directions before it bounced on en route for its target. An archer's head

144

disappeared in a spray of blood, bone, and brains, his lifeless body cart-wheeling through the ranks like a giant rag doll.

"By the bowels of the saints!" one of the archers exclaimed. "That was Roger Hunt from Lancastershire. He owes me a shilling from dicing!"

Denzel laughed, "It seems his luck today is as poor as when he throws dice!"

"He won't be making good on his debt now, I'll wager!" another man chimed in.

Hedyn's eyes were as big as plates. He had seen a man decapitated, an Englishman, and his mates made jokes of it. *Has war made my friends so callous?*

"Keep your heads, lads, and nock a bodkin," William called out. "There is Lord Erpingham. Now we will provoke the French into moving." The old knight strode quickly out in the field in front of the line where all could see him. He tossed a baton high in the air to draw the attention of all the archers.

"Now strike!" The old knight bellowed at the top of his lungs.

In unison, five thousand archers muscled bow cords to their ears and launched arrows high in the air toward the French lines. It was a long shot, so the high-arching arrows took several seconds to ascend before they started their deadly fall to earth. Hedyn could see a faint shadow that drifted across the wheat field created by the mass of five thousand feathered missiles. *Like a great flock of starlings*, he thought.

Before the first arrows began to thud into men and horses and to clang against armor, the archers were sending more arrows on their way, each man shooting at his own pace. Within a minute, 60,000 arrows were in the air or scattered across the battlefield. Some in dirt, some in men.

The arrow storm had its intended effect. Trumpets sounded, drums thumped, and the French line finally came to life.

"We are in for it now, lads," William said to no one in particular.

Mounted knights appeared on each side of the French formation, as the main line of armored men on foot began to move forward. The heavy armor and thick mud made them seem slow and clumsy.

"Put your arrows on the cavalry, lads. They will try to break our archers on the flanks," the ventenar instructed. "Help our mates on the flanks. Broadheads into horse flesh. If a horse goes down, the knight will go too." Hedyn hated to see the horses killed, but he knew that the highly trained animals were as much a weapon as the lances and swords that each of the knights pointed at his comrades.

From where he stood near the center of the line, Hedyn watched in awe as the French cavalry thundered toward the English flanks on either side of him. The air behind each of the big coursers filled with clods as pounding hoofs splattered the black mud.

The archers did not falter behind their wooden stakes but poured the bodkins and broadhead arrows into the mass of horses and men. Some began to fall as arrows found chinks in armor or were embedded in screaming horses. Some slowed and galloped back as it became too perilous near the archers and their stakes. A few stalwarts made it to the line of bowmen and discovered that the horses slowed or stopped, refusing to gallop into the protective barricade of stakes. These men were pulled from their mounts and killed by swarms of angry archers.

One man, a great nobleman in the finest armor, tumbled from his horse headlong as the animal impaled itself on a stake. Even from where Hedyn stood, the splash of red blood stood out on the bleak, muddy field. The man never had a chance to rise from his fall, killed where he lay.

"I knew these stakes were a good scheme the minute King Henry had us cut 'em back in Corbie!" Denzel said, almost as confidently as if he had devised the idea himself. The men rolled their eyes and laughed at him. He smiled sheepishly.

Panicked war-horses, some rider-less, crashed back through the oncoming French line, sending men-at-arms tumbling and scattering to make way. The line slowed, but regrouped and slogged on through the mud.

The French line began to change. It became bunched and irregular. The French knights instinctively crowded to the center to avoid the deadly arrows streaming from the English flanks. The archers stood behind their stakes and shot as fast as arrows could be nocked. The visibility of King Henry's banners at the center of the line reinforced this movement toward the center. The French knights were not disciplined enough to remain where the battle plan required. The line slowly transformed into a blunt wedge, which only presented more targets to the busy archers. The crowding made it much more difficult to wield lances and swords.

"Shoot, shoot! Pour it on, lads! Pour it on!" William screamed in a voice that Hedyn had never heard before. It seemed a mixture of terror, excitement, and merriment, almost like the voice of a boy involved in some risky prank. The arrows at the men's feet were long gone, and now each man shot the arrows in the extra bundles that Hedyn delivered before the fight. One hundred and twenty thousand arrows were gone, and still the French came.

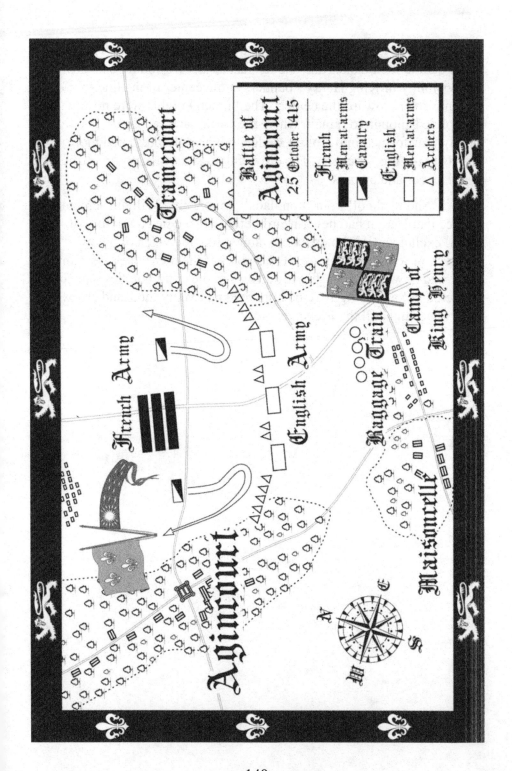

Battle of
Agincourt
25 October 1415

French
Men-at-arms
Cavalry

English
Men-at-arms
△ Archers

Tramecourt

French Army

Agincourt

English Army

Baggage Train

Camp of King Henry

Maisoncelle

N E S W

# CHAPTER TWENTY FIVE

**Agincourt, France**
**25 October 1415**

"Arrows, boy! Bring more arrows!" Whitwell shouted above the clamor of voices and the clang of metal that roared like a fierce wind from the French lines.

Hedyn stood transfixed as he watched the massive French juggernaut move clumsily in the mud, almost to the English lines. The gray, metallic line of eight thousand knights stretched as far as he could see to his right and left, like a single evil organism. A second line of armored men followed the first. To Hedyn, it seemed as if every sword and every lance came for him alone.

Whitwell's shouts broke his trance. "Don't stand there with your mouth open, boy! We're almost out of arrows."

"But I've issued out all of our sheaves!"

"Then go to the baggage train and look for more. Go now!" Whitwell gave him a swift shove to get him moving.

Hedyn turned quickly and crashed into a stake. The impact bounced him to the muddy ground. His bow slammed painfully into the back of his helmet. He scrambled to his feet and sprinted to the rear. Archers all along the line of battle screamed for more arrows.

The king's pennant fluttered in the light wind, but Hedyn could not see Henry among the sea of knights who made up his lifeguard. He pushed through the crush of men that made up the rear ranks, then wove his way through the pages and servants who danced anxiously, trying desperately to keep their masters in sight from their vantage points behind the lines.

A score of priests knelt in a circle of prayer. Their sodden robes blended with the morass that had once been a wheat field. It made them seem as if they were almost a part of the muddy earth. Hedyn slid in the mire to avoid the kneeling men and fell on a startled Father Stephen. Stephen held the boy still while he finished his prayer.

"Remember us, oh Lord. Our enemies are gathered together and boast themselves in their excellence. Destroy their strength and scatter them that they may understand, because there is none other that fighteth for us, but only Thou, our God. Amen."

Stephen released the squirming boy. "Son of Jago! Christ in heaven, boy. Did you come to join us in prayer for our king's victory?"

Hedyn regained his feet. "Nay, Father Stephen. We are out of arrows. My ventenar has sent me to fetch more." His oversized helmet sat askew on his head, and black mud clogged the iron links of his mail shirt.

"Then you must avoid this crowd of men. Pass through on our army's left." Father Stephen pointed to the woods. "Go yonder that way and skirt the edge of the wood. It will lead you to Maisoncelle where lies the baggage train. Make haste, boy!"

Hedyn dashed to the trees, dodging men and horses, although there were fewer to avoid as he distanced himself from the chaos of the front lines. He neared the wood and could see the towers of Agincourt Castle rising above the trees in the distance. The wood reminded him of those in Altarnon and gave him a sense of familiarity and security. The trees were widely spaced, and the forest floor seemed smooth and manicured. All branches and twigs that fell from the trees found their way into the hearths of the manor folk. The villagers' grazing cows, pigs, and sheep never allowed undergrowth to flourish.

A hint of metallic gray flashed from behind a giant oak. Hedyn moved cautiously around the trunk of the great tree and found himself face to face with a crouching Jan Tregeagle. Both were startled to see the other.

"You, villein's son. Why are you here spying on me?"

"I, I am not spying on you. I've been sent by my ventenar to the baggage train to fetch more arrows."

"Whitwell be damned! You are here spying on me just as you were at Harfleur, you little whelp!"

Tregeagle rose to his feet. He had discarded his helmet and much of his armor. The man loomed over Hedyn as the boy retreated a few steps.

"You should be on line. King Henry needs every man to meet the French."

Hedyn hoped his outrage would make him back away. It did not work. Tregeagle moved closer.

"You saw the French army. We are outnumbered five to one. They will kill the English to the last man, but they will not find me among them. I'll not die for Henry's vanity!"

Tregeagle looked around as though searching for a path of escape. "I'd sell my soul to the devil himself if I could be away from here and back in Cornwall."

The boy bristled at the thought of Tregeagle abandoning his post and fellow Altarnon men. He found the courage that had escaped him when Tregeagle last threatened him.

"You are a coward and a traitor to King Henry! Sir John shall know of this."

Hedyn turned to run, but Tregeagle grabbed the loose bow case on the boy's back. Hedyn could find no traction on the slick ground. Tregeagle pulled him from his feet. His helmet tumbled away. His mouth and nose filled with loamy soil as he crashed to the forest floor. A heavy, armored knee pushed against his back and a sharp blade pressed to his neck.

"You will tell no one except Saint Peter after I slit your throat, you worthless little tord!" Tregeagle snarled.

A woman's shriek pierced through the trees. A swelling of shouts and screams emanated from the direction of Maisoncelle.

A clear, distant voice shouted a warning. "The French! The French are attacking from our rear!"

Tregeagle's fear of the French was greater than his rage at the boy. The man jumped to his feet and stared wild-eyed in the direction of the screams. Hedyn scrambled away from his captor. A woman and small boy appeared through the trees. They scrambled by without a word. Close behind them followed an archer who bled heavily from a wound on the side of his head.

"We are attacked from the rear! The French have fallen on the baggage train and are killing everyone!" The wounded man stumbled on for the front line. Two wagoners dodged trees as they ran.

"Why are you running away?" Hedyn demanded.

"Because we can't fly away, you simpleton!" the older of the two shouted over his shoulder when he hurried passed.

Without a word, Tregeagle turned and fled in the direction of the village of Agincourt, away from the battlefield and away from the killing at the train.

Hedyn stood for a moment trying to decide what to do. His first thought was to run and warn William Whitwell of the French attack, but he realized that others would have already warned King Henry and his commanders. Besides, Whitwell had a larger threat to his front. Then Hedyn remembered that Squire John had been left with a small force to defend the baggage train. He stood, jammed on his helmet, and ran toward the screams to help his friend.

*   *   *

Chaos enveloped the baggage train. Hedyn dodged several loose horses that galloped about in panic. He wondered if El was safe. Several hundred French peasants, led by a handful of men-at-arms, rampaged through the wagons and carts. The screams of the fleeing English were drowned by the laughter and catcalls of the mob. The peasants, mostly villeins from the nearby manors, were armed with scythes, axes, and pitchforks. Hardly weapons of war, the tools were yet deadly. Scores of wagoners, boys, and servants lay like lifeless heaps of rags where they had been slain. Most of the mob sought English plunder more than English blood. Their attention quickly shifted to pillaging the wagons.

One ragged French peasant emerged from the king's ornate wagon wearing a golden crown and a purple robe around his shoulders. The mob quickly overcame him and took his newfound treasure. The crowd hardly noticed Hedyn when he skirted the chaos and moved on.

The boy desperately scanned the scene for his friend. At last he could see John and three archers pinned against the side of large wagon. John sliced the air with his sword to keep an armored man and six peasants at bay. The archers, out of arrows, stood with him and desperately defended themselves with short swords and poleaxes.

Hedyn took his bow from its case. He had never been able to string his new bow on the first try, but with one swift movement he bent the bow and strung the cord.

"Arrows!" He realized he had no arrows and began a frantic search. He found a dead archer whose head had been cleaved with an ax early in the fight. He tugged at the dead man's bloody arrow bag until it came from his lifeless shoulder.

"Please God, let there be arrows!" he pleaded. The bag held six arrows, but half were broken from the man's fall. Three would have to serve.

Hedyn nocked and pulled the white goose feathers all the way back to his ear, just as his father had taught him. The broadhead sailed a hundred paces, glanced off the breastplate of the man-at-arms, and sank into the neck of a peasant. The shocked man dropped his ax and fell to the ground. Even at that distance Hedyn heard the clang of the steel arrowhead on armor and a sickening thud when it found the peasant's flesh.

The French knight saw the geyser of blood from his comrade's killing wound and began looking for this new threat. By the time he turned and faced Hedyn, the boy had nocked, sighted, and loosed his second arrow. The bodkin struck square, penetrated the armor, and sliced into the man's heart. The dying knight grabbed the arrow shaft, opened his mouth as though to speak, then sank to his knees.

A third arrow punched through the gut of the tallest peasant just as the tattered man realized that his leader was down. He screamed and crumpled to the ground in a heap. The remaining four lost all resolve and fled out of Hedyn's range. They soon joined the wild melee of plunder elsewhere in the train. It was all over in less than twenty seconds.

Hedyn fell to his hands and knees and vomited into the mud.

# CHAPTER TWENTY SIX

**Maisoncelle, France**
**25 October 1415**

The rush of adrenaline, three dead Frenchmen, and the sudden end to the fight turned Hedyn's stomach inside out. Squire John and his comrades were quickly by his side. John helped him to his feet.

"Hedyn, you have saved us! I thought you could not draw your bow. Where did you find the strength?"

Hedyn could not answer.

An archer put his hand on the boy's shoulder. "Aye. No shame, boy. I too emptied me belly with the first man I killed. You are a true archer this day, lad."

A second archer gave the two boys a gentle push. "We can congratulate one another when the day is won. We must flee before this mob takes interest in us again."

As they turned and trotted away, the clamor of six hundred looting peasants still echoed across the field and on to the Village of Maisoncelle.

When Hedyn left the front lines, he was sure that his dirty, starving army was doomed. But when they made their way back to the front, he found that his comrades were not all dead or scattered. The sounds of battle were fading, and the same milling mob of non-combatants still clogged the way forward. Then he started to see dead men. Dead Frenchmen, more than he could ever count, were behind the lines where there had been no fighting. Squire John saw them too and hesitated as they stepped over a body. The dead man lay on his back. His eyes were open, and his gaping mouth was a pool of blood.

"Look at the elaborate armor on this man. He was a noble or a great knight." The squire was puzzled. "See how he has taken off his helmet and his gauntlets? Under the rules of chivalry, he has surrendered and asked for quarter. Even so, for some reason, he was killed."

Hedyn led Squire John to where the Altarnon men-at-arms were posted near the center of the line. Sir John was in animated conversation with another knight when his son tugged at his elbow. He held his helmet under his arm. Despite the cool air, his thinning hair was plastered with sweat against his head. Sir John turned.

"Praise Christ in Heaven! You are safe." The two embraced clumsily in their mud-smeared armor. "Was it as bad at the baggage train as I have heard? The king has already sent men to retake it."

"Aye, it was. If it had not been for Hedyn and his bow, I surely would have been slain. He killed three Frenchmen!"

Sir John looked down at Hedyn. "Three Frenchmen you say? That is quite a feat. Not unlike your father, who saved my skin at Shrewsbury these many years ago."

Hedyn winced at the mention of the dead Frenchmen. He pretended a smile but said nothing. He felt relieved that his friend was safe, but could find no joy in his triumph. The boy changed the subject.

"Sir John, if I may tell you something? I found Jan Tregeagle hiding in the wood. He has deserted the army."

"Tregeagle, that rogue! He disappeared when the French cavalry made their charge. I wondered what became of him. I suspect he also lied when he claimed he became separated from us at Harfleur. He will never show his face in Altarnon again, or risk hanging." Sir John paused.

"Never mind Tregeagle. God has shown his mercy and his love for King Henry this day. The French are crushed."

Sir John led the boys in front of the line so they could see the battlefield. The last of the French army was in retreat and clearing the road to Calais. Thousands of spent arrows bristled from the ground as if the field had sprouted a deadly harvest. Dead horses and men killed by the showers of arrows dotted the broad field, but the carnage in front of the English lines shocked Hedyn. Thousands of dead Frenchmen lay in thick rows where they had been slain. The piles were deepest in front of the banners of the English commanders. There, over-confident Frenchmen sought to capture a worthy ransom. He could see very few Englishmen on the ground.

155

"God has surely granted us a victory against the greatest odds. The French dead number more than our entire army." Squire John said breathlessly.

"Ah, my ventenar!" Sir John greeted Whitwell as he approached. "I saw you among the enemy wielding your poleaxe and doing great slaughter. How do my other archers fare?"

"All well except one man. He took a lance thrust to the thigh, but I believe he will survive to see Cornwall again."

"Excellent! Take this young archer with you and see to your men. Young Hedyn has proved his mettle this day."

Hedyn told Whitwell what occurred at the baggage train while they walked to rejoin the other archers. He tried to minimize his success. The man listened in silence, and then said, "You did your duty, but you are right to do no boasting of killing other men. You and God must sort that out between the two of you."

Whitwell explained to Hedyn how the battle played out. The French, in their masses, expected an easy victory against a smaller, starving foe. But confidence caused them to compete to be on the front line, each in search of glory and rich Englishmen to capture for ransom. But the deep mud and heavy armor made them clumsy and sluggish. The crowded ranks left no room to swing swords or thrust lances. As those in the front line were struck down, the later ranks stumbled upon the dead as they were crowded from the rear. The English ranks were less compact so the men-at-arms could wield their blades.

"Aye, when we ran out of arrows, we archers went in with swords and poleaxes. We are very nimble without armor to slow us. It was an easy task to knock an armored man down in the mud and find a place between armor plates to thrust a sword. Some men would simply open a screaming Frenchman's visor and plunge a dagger through his eye and into his brain. I thank God that you were not here to see it."

Whitwell fell silent. Hedyn could tell that he was replaying the horror in his mind. After a few minutes Hedyn asked, "Ventenar, what of the dead men behind the lines?"

"A sad business, that. Hundreds of the French asked for quarter, and many Englishmen were happy to grant it in anticipation of a ransom from the families of those men. But then it looked as though the French were preparing for another attack, and we heard that there was an attack from our rear."

"The baggage train?" Hedyn asked.

"Aye, the baggage. The king was afraid the prisoners would take up the arms scattered on the field and join the attack. He ordered them all killed. But when it was clear there was to be no new attack on the front, and that the attack on the train was only a great mob of villeins, Henry ordered a halt to the slaughter. Yet, many hundreds were slain. He was justified in his order, but it was a sad business just the same."

Hedyn stopped Whitwell and faced him. "Ventenar, do you still believe that God does not show his favor to kings and nations?"

"After what I have witnessed this day, I know not. All I know is that Christ showed his mercy to me today. I pray to all that is holy that he will forgive me for the things that I did."

\* \* \*

Raucous laughter roared from the king's pavilion. Henry, his closest lieutenants, and the most noble of the French captives shared food and wine in the great tent. Their celebration had gone deep into the night. The English celebrated their victory; the French captives celebrated survival.

Hedyn and the Altarnon archers huddled around the trunk of a big tree in the little village of Maisoncelle. They shared a single blanket and canvas oilcloth. They were close enough to hear the laughter and see the shadows of men cast by lamps on the pavilion's canvas walls. The cold damp air sucked the feeling from their shivering limbs.

"I'm glad some men are warm and have full bellies," a muffled voice came from beneath the blanket.

Another responded, "Aye, but I wish they would take their celebration elsewhere so we can get some sleep."

Denzel Crocker offered, "Not to worry. On the morrow we will be on the road to Calais where we will fill our bellies at last. I knew it was the best of plans to march overland to Calais."

The other men all moaned in unison at Denzel's claim.

Hedyn heard shuffling and a whisper on the other side of their scanty shelter.

"Hedyn, Hedyn are you beneath there?"

"I am here." Hedyn flipped the corner of the blanket from his head. The sudden rush of cold air chased the pent-up smell of dried blood and unwashed men from his nose. He found Squire John bending low and peering into the dark.

"So you are. Come with me."

Hedyn shivered as he emerged and followed Squire John out of earshot of the others.

"I brought you this. I'm sorry there is so little, and not enough to divide between all the men. I saved it from the meager meal that my father shared with me."

Squire John handed Hedyn a chunk of stale brown bread and an overripe pear. Hedyn took the food then looked up at John.

"I am very grateful; it is more than I have had to eat in many days."

"Hedyn, it is I that should be grateful. You have saved me twice. I would have died with Roger if you had not cared for me when I was ill. And if you had not found me at the baggage, I surely would have been slain. You could have chosen to do neither of these things.

We were good friends once. Our different stations in life did not separate us as little children. But I went away for my training as squire and returned believing that my inheritance should make me a tyrant to you. And to Roger Kelnystok too for that matter."

"Squire, you do not have to. . ."

"Hear me out. I will be lord of the manor someday, and you shall always work the land. But that does not require that I treat you as I have. I've learned more than the ways of war on this campaign. I understand now that I must have a loyalty to you just as you have to me. I promise that you will always be treated fairly and will never be in need as long as you are under my charge.

158

I must return to my father now. We will be marching very early on the morrow. It will be a short march to Calais, and from there we will sail back to Cornwall soon."

Hedyn watched Squire John as he turned and melted into the dark night. He wanted to stop him and tell him that he had never stopped being his friend, no matter how he had been treated. As he gobbled the bread, he hefted the precious fruit in his free hand. He reckoned that it was just large enough for every archer under the blanket to have at least one bite.

# EPILOGE

Jan Tregeagle never returned to Altarnon. A stranger passed through the parish not long before Sir John and his company returned. Tregeagle's cottage was found deserted that day, his wife and children gone. The miller's wife told the manor folk that she had heard that Jan Tregeagle was living in Bodmin Town on the far side of Fowey Moor.

Thomas Kelnystok recovered in body but not in spirit. He met Sir John Trelawny's company on the road into Altarnon when they returned. His cheerless eyes scanned the men as though he were looking for a certain face—a face that he knew could not be among them. For years after his return, he was content to sit at the butts for hours, watching the village boys practice with longbow and arrow.

Jago, Guenbrith, and Tressa were waiting with the other manor folk to see their Agincourt heroes return home. The company rode across the packhorse bridge over Penpont Waters to Saint Nonna's Church. It seemed as if every person in the parish was there to welcome them. Father Leofric said a long, sleepy prayer in Latin. Sir John praised his men and said a few words of thanks to those gathered. To everyone's surprise, Sir John then called Jago and his family forward and led them into the church to Saint Nonna's ancient altar.

The whole parish crowded in behind them, curious to see what would befall the lowly villeins. The knight recounted Hedyn's bravery and loyalty in the face of disease and sword and how his son's life was saved twice over by the actions of the young serf.

"Young Hedyn, son of Jago, you have a heart that is true. Your loyalty has brought you freedom. You are free from your service," Sir John announced. And there, in the presence of God, he released Jago, Guenbrith, Hedyn, and Tressa from their bonds. They were freemen, no longer villeins tied to the land. He invited Jago to move his family to the farm that had once been worked by Jan Tregeagle and live there without rent for as long as he should live. A satisfied Squire John stood by his father's side and smiled at Hedyn.

Sir John did not sell El with the rest of the extra horses after their return from France. Squire John told him the story of how the old horse had found Hedyn and William and carried them to safety. El was allowed to spend the last of her days grazing peacefully with the

160

Trelawny coursers, never again carrying a burden on her back. Hedyn visited her almost every day.

Sir John Trelawny went on to serve King Henry V in later campaigns in France. He so distinguished himself in battle that Henry granted him a coat of arms, a pension for life, and had inscribed over the gate to the nearby town of Dunheved the following:

## HE THAT WOULD DO OUGHT FOR ME

## LET HYM LOVE WELL SIR JOHN TRELAWNIE

After Sir John's passing, Squire John received his knighthood and inherited his father's manor at Altarnon. The Trelawnys remain one of the most ancient and distinguished families of Cornwall to this day.

William Whitwell of Devon remained in Sir John's service until the company returned to Altarnon. He collected his wages and moved on. The other archers respected him for his skill and leadership, but his aloofness had made him no lasting friends among the Altarnon men. They showed no regret when he left them. Whitwell sought out Hedyn before he took his leave.

"I have saved this for you, lad," he told the boy.

Whitwell held out an ivory-handled dagger, taken from a French nobleman on the killing fields of Agincourt. The snow-white handle was inlaid with a gold cross and fleur-de-les.

"It is marvelous. I shall always treasure it. Shall you return home to Devonshire now?" Hedyn asked.

"Nay. There is nothing there for me. I have no skills except monk or archer, and I shall never again wear the robes. I shall find some other knight whom I can serve. There will always be need for soldiers."

Hedyn was reluctant to see him go. "Will you not stay in Altarnon for a short time at least?"

"Nay, I must be on my way. *Duw genes*, Hedyn Archer's Son."

"God be with you too, William Whitwell." The boy watched as the big archer started down the sunken lane that led to London. He realized that he was finally no longer a nameless villein's son.

For many months after his return, Hedyn seldom smiled or shared mirth with family or friends. He somehow thought that happiness was disloyal to the grief that he felt for Roger, Lawrence, and other lost friends who were in lonely, anonymous graves at Harfleur. Only through prayer did his sadness finally subside. Christ brought him the understanding that his duty was to the living, not to the dead.

But he never shook the demons that came to him in his sleep. Each night was a dreamy torment of charging black knights, clouds of arrows, blood, and lifeless bodies. Only his bride knew of his suffering. The ivory-handled dagger remained hidden under his sleeping mat. It seemed the only thing to bring him at least a tiny bit of refuge from his dread of the night. Even as an old man, fifty years after Agincourt, the dreams sometimes came to torture him.

Hedyn Archerson became the Trelawny family's most trusted tenant. When the younger John inherited the lands, Hedyn became steward and managed much of the manor affairs when the lord was absent. But Hedyn never again followed his knight into battle. He left the little village of Altarnon only when manor business demanded. The wanderlust that had burned in him as a child was extinguished on a muddy wheat field at Agincourt. He was content to live out his days on the rolling fields of home.

William's story left a lasting impression on Hedyn. He no longer accepted the Church, or rumors, or even the words of his master at face value. His natural curiosity sharpened and he began to think for himself in all things. He convinced Father Stephen to teach him to read under the guise of being a better steward for his master, but his quest for truth expanded far beyond the business of Altarnon Manor. On a journey to Dunheved to sell his master's wool one season, he purchased a forbidden English copy of the four Gospels. He read it in secret whenever he felt it was safe to do so. It was many years before even his wife knew that it was carefully hidden away in their tiny cottage.

In later life, small boys would sometimes shyly approach the gray-haired old man and ask, "Hedyn Archerson, you were there? You were with Henry at Agincourt?" They would puff themselves up and try to appear older as they clutched their little bows.

He would sigh and respond, "Aye. I was there. I was at Agincourt."

But he told only stories that made him laugh or made him happy or brought him pride.  He told no tales that brought him sadness.

## THE END

# HISTORICAL NOTES

First and foremost, this is a work of fiction. Hedyn, Roger, William, Denzel, and many others are all products of my imagination. The times and places in which these characters live, however, are very real. I've strived to be true to the history in my descriptions of the siege of Harfleur, the march to Calais, and the Battle of Agincourt. However, in some instances I've filled gaps in the narrative where mundane historical details were not available.

Some of the characters are based on real people, such as Sir John Trelawny. Altarnon Parish in Cornwall was the original seat of the Trelawny family. Sir John (born 1386) was the coroner for Cornwall and also represented the county in Parliament. A Parliamentary biography of Sir John Trelawny reveals:

> "*And it was certainly this John Trelawny who excelled himself in France and, according to family tradition, fought at Agincourt. In August 1415 he received letters of protection to safeguard his interests while he was overseas in the retinue of Edward, Lord Courtenay, the earl of Devon's heir, who did indeed combat the French on that field; and within two years he had been knighted. In March 1417 he was preparing to go abroad again, this time under the command of the duke of Exeter. While on military service in Normandy, Trelawny clearly could not carry out his duties as coroner in Cornwall, so the Crown ordered the sheriff to hold a fresh election to provide a replacement. At Gisors on 27 Sept. 1419, now as a 'King's knight', he was granted £20 p.a. as an annuity from the coinage of tin in Cornwall.*"[1]

I regret to say that Squire John, although a real person, was not born until five years after the Battle of Agincourt. I've taken extreme historical liberties and advanced him in age so he could share this adventure with his father and my fictional Hedyn.

---

[1] http://www.historyofparliamentonline.org/volume/1386-1421/member/trelawny-john-ii

Saint Nonna's Church still stands in Altarnon (now spelled Altarnun), although it was remodeled in the 16th century using stone and timbers from the abandoned Trelawny manor house. Saint Nonna's Well still flows to this day, but you will have to search to find it, as it is hidden in a clump of trees in a sheep pasture. The stone packhorse bridge over Penpont Water that is mentioned in the story is as sturdy now as when it was built seven hundred years ago. I had the privilege of visiting Cornwall and Devonshire in 2012 and drove the route that my fictional company of archers would have traversed from Altarnon to Plymouth. Seeing the village of Altarnon and traveling the green countryside and ancient narrow lanes provided an insight I could never have gained from maps or photographs.

I have tried to present historical figures such as King Henry and Sir Thomas Erpingham as true to history as possible. Although I have created a few scenes involving Sir Thomas, I have written those scenes in a way that does not contradict historical records about his role in the Agincourt Campaign.

I did not have to exaggerate the effects of disease on the English army during the Siege of Harfleur. The flux spread like wildfire through the army. It this case, it was thought to have been caused by a virulent strain of the bacterium *shingella dysenteriae*. It spread through food and water supplies coming in contact with infected human waste. The concept of germs and infection sources were unknown at the time. Nobles and commoners alike perished in great numbers during the siege. Most of those who did not succumb suffered from chronic dysentery for the entire campaign. Toward the end of the siege, King Henry began to send home those men who were too sick with the flux to continue in the field, further depleting the ranks of his army.

I've described the Battle of Agincourt only as far as Hedyn would have personally observed it. There were a great many boys and young men who accompanied the army as non-combatants, and those who were left at the baggage train in Maisoncelle paid a terrible toll. The number killed by the French peasants is not known, but it could have easily been as high as the number of soldiers killed in the line of battle.

Readers in Cornwall will recognize the name Jan Tregeagle. In Cornish folklore, Jan Tregeagle was a magistrate who lived in Bodmin on the edge of the moor. He was an underhanded swindler who engaged in all kinds of evil deeds to amass his wealth.  He is said to have murdered his wife and children and later made a pact with the devil.  He is sometimes called the "Cornish Doctor Foust."  Although the legend has grown through the ages, it is thought that Tregeagle really existed and lived in early 17th century Cornwall.  Who is to say that he did not have an equally evil distant grandfather by the same name?  When I was developing the antagonist for this story, I stumbled upon this legend and my villain became Jan Tregeagle.

Many of the Cornish names in the story were common at the time and come from a list of names recorded in the Bodmin Manumissions in the 10th century, including Hedyn, Denzel, Guenbrith, and others. Novelist Daphne Du Maurier describes an area just south of Altarnon called Twelve Men's Moor.  Records put down in 1285 list Thomas Kelnystok as one of twelve men who were given rights to cultivate that land.[2]  I've use that name for one of my secondary characters, as I suspect his descendent still farmed the manors around Altarnon at the time of my story in 1415.  Du Maurier's most famous novel, *The Jamaica Inn*, is set just four miles from Altarnon.  The inn by that name still stands to this day.

M. E. Hubbs
Huntsville, Alabama
2014

---

[2] Trewin, J.C. Editor, The West Country Book. Webb & Bowyer (1981) P 53

# SUGGESTED READING

There are many publications on the Battle of Agincourt available. Some are better than others. I used scores of references to develop the historical parts of this story. The following texts are some of the books that I found helpful when I studied the Agincourt Campaign, the longbow, and life in medieval England.

*Agincourt: Henry V and the Battle That Made England*, by Juliet Barker: Little, Brown and Company (2006)

*Agincourt 1415: Triumph against the odds*, by Matthew Bennett: Osprey Publishing (1991)

*The Time Traveler's Guide to Medieval England: A Handbook for Visitors to the Fourteenth Century*, by Ian Mortimer: Touchstone (2009) **(Authors Note: Some of the discussions of sexuality and bodily functions in this publication may not be suitable for young children!)**

*1381: The Peel Affinity: An English Knight's Household in the Fourteenth Century*, by La Belle Compagnie: (2006)

*The Crooked Stick: A History of the Longbow*, Hugh D. H. Soar: Westholme Publishing (November 1, 2004)

*The Longbow*, by Mike Loades, illustrated by Peter Dennis: Osprey Publishing (2013)

*English Longbowman 1330-1515*, by Clive Bartlett, illustrated by Gerry Embleton: Osprey Publishing (1995)

# GLOSSARY

**Abbot** - Meaning "father." The title given to the monk who was in charge of a monastery.

**Altarnon** - Altarnun (modern spelling) is a village and civil parish in Cornwall, England. It takes its name from the Altar of St. Nonna. It is located on the northeastern edge of Bodmin Moor and about seven miles west of Launceston. During the Middle Ages, the parish of Altarnon included the village of Penpont, where St. Nonna's Church stood and the hamlets Treween and Trewint.

**Apogee** – The point farthest from the earth a missile reaches before it begins to fall back to earth.

**Arbalest** - A type of crossbow.

**Aventail** - A curtain of chain mail attached to the sides of a helmet that extends to cover the throat, neck, and shoulders.

**Barbican** - A fortification designed to protect a gate or other entranceway into city or castle walls.

**Bascinet** - An open-faced military helmet with a pointed apex to the skull, which extended downward at the rear and sides to afford protection for the neck. A mail curtain called an aventail was usually attached to the lower edge of the helmet to protect the throat, neck, and shoulders. Some bascinets, especially those worn by knights in full armor, also had a visor.

**Benedictine** – A member of a Christian order of monks and nuns founded by St. Benedict of Nursia in AD 529.

**Bloody Flux** - Acute diarrhea caused by an infection by bacteria or amoebas, spread through contamination of food and water by infected fecal matter. Symptoms: (Bacillary) After 1-6 days incubation: watery stools, fever, cramps, dehydration. In advanced stages: bloody stools, meningitis, conjunctivitis, and arthritis. (Amebic) Acute form: watery, bloody stools, cramps, fever, weakness. Either form can be fatal if not treated. The bloody flux killed more men in medieval armies than combat with the enemy.

**Bodkin** - A long, pointed arrowhead with no barbs which was designed to penetrate mail and armor.

**Brais** - A man's under pants, usually made of linen.

**British Sea** - The medieval name for the English Channel.

**Broadhead** - A barbed arrowhead designed to inflict maximum damage to flesh.

**Brown Willy** - A hill mass in Bodmin Moor that is the highest point in Cornwall.

**Calais** - A fortified port town in northern France that was held by the English from AD1360 - AD1558.

**Crapaud** - French for frog.

**Chain mail** - Simply called "mail" during the Middle Ages. This was a system of interlocking steel rings made into garments to protect the body from edged weapons.

**Cistercian** – A member of an austere Christian order of monks and nuns founded by reformist Benedictines in AD1098.

**Circuitor** -The title of the monk at a priory or monastery who was in charge of keeping order.

**Cog** - A small single-masted ship that was common in the Middle Ages.

**Coif** - Cloth headwear that was form fitted to the head and tied under the chin. Usually made of linen.

**Cotehardie** - A form-fitting, coat-like garment that buttons up the front and on the lower arms. They generally extended down to the upper thighs.

**Cotter** - Also known as a cottager. Cotters were ranked below a villein in the social hierarchy of a manor, holding a cottage, garden, and just enough land to feed a family. In England this would have been between about 1 and 5 acres.

**Crossbow -** A shoulder-held weapon made with a stock and small bow attached crosswise to the end. The small bow was very powerful and could launch a short arrow (called a quarrel) to great distances.

**Cutpurse** - A thief or pickpocket.

**Dauphin -** The title for the prince who was heir to the French throne.

**Doublet** - A short, fitted outer garment, usually expensively decorated and worn by the upper classes.

**DuwGenes** – Cornish for "God be with you."

**Dunheved** - The old English name for Launceston, Cornwall.

**Fairing** - A small, sweet biscuit or cookie flavored with ginger. The term fairing originated in the 13th century to describe small, sweet treats that could be purchased at fairs. In Cornwall, the term eventually evolved to describe the ginger biscuits that are still popular there today.

**Fascines** - A tight bundle of sticks, bound together and used in military operations for filling in marshy ground or other obstacles and for strengthening the sides of embankments, ditches, or trenches.

**Fowey Moor** - The old name for Bodmin Moor, it was named for the River Fowey that rises in the moor.

**Gambeson** - A heavy garment of many layers of linen and padding, usually quilted together. It was the simplest type of armor, worn alone or worn under mail for additional protection.

**Goat's Foot** - A hinged metal lever used to cock a crossbow.

**Gonne** -Medieval spelling and pronunciation for cannon.

**Great Mortality** - The bubonic plague. Also known as the "Black Death."

**Hauberk** - A mail garment worn on the upper body to protect the torso and arms from sword and ax blows.

**Horse Bread** - This is coarse bread made of barley or rye flour and ground, dried peas or beans. It is called horse bread because wealthy men fed it to their horses. This bread was a staple in the lower-class diet.

**Hosen** - These were sometimes called chausers and were the trousers of the era. Each leg wore a separate hosen that came up to the top of the thigh. Each one was tied to the brais (underwear) to keep them up.

**L'Anglais** – French for "The English."

**Lollard** - (Lollardy, Lollardism) This was a political and religious movement that existed from the mid-14th century to the English Reformation. The term "Lollard" refers to the followers of John Wycliffe, a prominent theologian who was dismissed from the

University of Oxford in 1381 for criticism of the Church. The Lollards' demands were primarily for adherence to Holy Scripture and reform of Western Christianity.

**Malted Barley** – This is the process of wetting un-winnowed grain, such as barley or wheat, and allowing it to germinate. After two to three days of germination, it is toasted to stop the process and to add flavor. Malted grains are the main ingredient for producing ale and beer.

**Mamm** - Cornish for mother

**Matins** - The dawn prayer service in a monastery, sometimes known as Prime or Lauds.

**Melee** – A noisy confused hand-to-hand fight involving a large number of people.

**Muskogyon** – Cornish for a mentally ill man.

**Oatcake** - A small, flat loaf of unleavened bread made from oat flour.

**Offal** – The intestines and other inedible or unpalatable parts of an animal that are discarded.

**Pavilion** - A large tent used by nobles or other high-ranking people. They were often very elaborately decorated.

**Palfrey** - A saddle or riding horse. Not as large or as powerful as a courser.

**Poleaxe** - A fearsome weapon that included an ax blade, spike, and hammer mounted on a five-foot pole.

**Popinjay** - A feathered target the size of a bird that was used for practice with bows and arrows in medieval times.

**Porridge** - A thick, hot food made from boiled, ground grains such as barley or wheat. Modern oatmeal and cream of wheat are types of porridge.

**Portagee** - Slang for Portuguese.

**Pottage** - A stew made of vegetables, grain, or meat, or a mixture of all three.

**Priory** - A monastic institution. Often established as a subsidiary of an abbey. Usually headed by a prior.

**Quarrel** - A short, stout arrow fired from a crossbow. Called a "bolt" in modern terminology.

**Quilted Jack** - See Gambeson.

**Rook** - A large black bird similar to a crow.

**Serf, Serfdom** - The term used for peasants under feudalism. It was a condition of modified slavery which developed in medieval Europe. Serfs who occupied a plot of land were required to work for the lord of the manor who owned that land, and in return were entitled to protection, justice, and the right to exploit certain fields within the manor to maintain their own subsistence. The manor formed the basic unit of feudal society and the lord of the manor and his serfs were bound legally, economically, and socially. Serfs formed the lowest social class of feudal society. The decline of serfdom in Western Europe has sometimes been attributed to the Great Mortality, which reached Europe in 1347.

**Surcoat** - A sleeveless overgarment, often used by military personnel to display family, feudal allegiance, or national identity.

**Target Butts** - Archery target set up in common areas of villages for archers to practice with their bows.

**Tas** - Cornish for father.

**Taw Taves Hwoer** - Cornish for "be quite sister."

**Tord** - Old English for feces.

**Tunic** - A simple pullover garment worn by the lower classes. Made of linen or wool, they came down to mid-thigh or below.

**Ventenar** - The leader of a contingent of archers, usually about twenty men. Similar to a sergeant in modern military organizations.

**Villein-** A villein was the most common type of serf in the Middle Ages. Villeins had more rights and higher status than cotters, but existed under a number of legal restrictions that differentiated them from freemen. Villeins generally rented small homes, with or without land. As part of the contract with the lord of the manor, they were expected to spend some of their time working on the lord's fields. The rest of their time was spent farming their own allotted plots for their own profit. Although they had some rights, they were not freemen and could not leave the manor or the service of their lord.

**Winnow** – The process of removing the outer husk from grain before it is milled for making bread.

**Yarn** – A story or tale.

## The Song of the Bow

What of the bow?
The bow was made in England:
Of true wood, of yew wood,
The wood of English bows;
So men who are free
Love the old yew tree
And the land where the yew tree grows.

What of the cord?
The cord was made in England:
A rough cord, a tough cord,
A cord that bowmen love;
So we'll drain our jacks
To the English flax
And the land where the hemp was wove.

What of the shaft?
The shaft was cut in England:
A long shaft, a strong shaft,
Barbed and trim and true;
So we'll drink all together
To the gray goose feather
And the land where the gray goose flew.

What of the men?
The men were bred in England:
The bowman--the yeoman--
The lads of dale and fell
Here's to you--and to you;
To the hearts that are true
And the land where the true hearts dwell.

Sir Arthur Conan Doyle
*The White Company*

If you enjoyed this book and would like to help others make an informed decision, please go to Amazon and/ or Goodreads and post a review.

The Archer's Son
on Amazon

Review on
Goodreads.com

The author would like to thank the Alabama Renaissance Festival (ARF), the Florence-Lauderdale Public Library and Bluewater Publications, who in partnership, have made The Archer's Son such a success. The Roundtable (Board of Governors) of the ARF took an interest in The Archer's Son early on and offered to help in promoting the story as both an educational and entertaining book for young readers. The Florence-Lauderdale Public Library provided an excellent facility for our "Archer's Son Launch Party" which the book launch was a part of. I appreciate that the library had enough faith in The Archer's Son to open the library for our use. And of course, without the resources of Bluewater Publications, Hedyn's story would never have been set in type.

The Florence-Lauderdale Public Library is located in the historic district of Florence, Alabama. Visit their website at: http://www.flpl.org.

The Alabama Resistance Festival is held each October It is a non-profit, free to the general public event. You can learn more about it at: www.alarenfaire.org.

Florence-Lauderdale
Public Library

ALARENFAIRE.ORG

# About the Aurthor

Mark Hubbs is an eleven year veteran of the U.S. Army Infantry. He left active duty in 1992 and retired from the Army Reserve in 2001. Since leaving active duty he worked as a historic preservation specialist and archaeologist for the US Army Space and Missile Defense Command. His work has taken him to several far flung islands in the Pacific where the fierce battles of World War II have left relics both above and below the surface of the corral sand.

Besides the extensive non-fiction writing that Mark does for his job, he has also written non-fiction for several history related magazines and journals. The Secret of Wattensaw Bayou is his first novel.

Mark has had a lifelong passion for history. This interest ranges from battles and leaders to the more mundane cultural and material history of the common people who were the real heroes of the past. History is more than anything else the story of ordinary people and how those people reacted to extraordinary circumstances. For almost four decades Mark has learned firsthand how the people of the past lived by participating in costumed living history programs at scores of American battlefields and historic sites.

Mark holds a Bachelor's in History from Henderson State University in Arkansas, a Masters in Environmental Management from Samford University in Birmingham, Alabama and a Masters in Archaeology from Leicester University in the United Kingdom.

Huntsville, Alabama has been home for Mark and his wife Phyllis since 1989. They have three children and five grandchildren.

To learn more about the author, visit his web site at http://www.MEHubbs.com.

MEHubbs.com

Bluewater Publications is a multi-faceted publishing company capable of meeting all of your reading and publishing needs. Our two-fold aim is to:

1) Provide the market with educationally enlightening and inspiring research and reading materials.

2) Make the opportunity of being published available to any author and or researcher who desire to be published.

We are passionate about preserving history; whether through the re-publishing of an out-of-print classic, or by publishing the research of historians and genealogists. Bluewater Publications is the *Peoples' Choice Publisher*.

For company information or information about how you can be published through Bluewater Publications, please visit:

**www.BluewaterPublications.com**

Also check Amazon.com to purchase any of the books that we publish.

*Confidently Preserving Our Past,*
Bluewater Publications.com

CPSIA information can be obtained
at www.ICGtesting.com
Printed in the USA
FSOW03n0653291116
27939FS